SHRI ADI SHANKARACHARYA'S

VAKYA VRITTI

Exhaustive Analysis of That Thou Art

Commentary by
Swami Chinmayananda

Central Chinmaya Mission Trust

Printed upto - March 2010 - 18,000 copies
Second Edition - November 2014 to April 2023 - 4,100 copies
Reprint - May 2024 - 700 copies

Published by:
Chinmaya Prakashan
The Publications Division of
Central Chinmaya Mission Trust
Sandeepany Sadhanalaya
Saki Vihar Road, Powai, Mumbai 400072, India
Tel.: +91-22-2803 4900
Email: ccmtpublications@chinmayamission.com
Website: www.chinmayamission.com

Distribution Centre in the USA:
Chinmaya Publications West
560 Bridgetown Pike
Feasterville, PA 19053-7240, USA
Tel.: (215) 396-0390, Fax: (215) 396-9710
Email: publications@chinmayamission.org
Website: www.chinmayapublications.com

Designed by: Chinmaya Kalpanam, Mumbai

Printed by: Trinity Academy, Mumbai

ISBN: 978-81-7597-665-8

Preface

Books that help us to open up and enter freely into the subtle world of thoughts dealt with and severally expounded in the scriptures, are called prakriyā books. Śaṅkara has authored many such elementary textbooks and prescribed them for the students of Vedānta. Each of these books has a different and distinct standard; each is meant for a different type of student.

The most elementary text of this type can be *Tattvabodha*. The topics dealt with and explained in *Tattvabodha* are again elaborated on a large canvas in *Ātmabodha*. These ideas discussed therein and vividly brought to us in these two texts of Vedānta, are spread in dazzling colours on the high walls and wide ceilings of the splendours of the palace of knowledge in Acārya's *Vivekacūḍamaṇi*.

The anxious teacher must have felt that though these three textbooks will introduce any student to a clear glimpse of the silent and peaceful fields of the advaita philosophy, they do not fully initiate him into the subtle mysteries and irresistible beauties of the mystic statements of the Vedas – the Mahāvākyas.

The Vedāntin accepts the four great statements of the Vedas as the Mahāvākyas. They define and declare the infinite Brahman; they advise the seekers upon the means of gaining that transcendental experience; they faithfully reflect the student's own direct moments of Realisation; they echo the thunderous roar of the seeker's confirmation of the Self.

'Consciousness is Brahman' (Prajñānam Brahma) is the definition of the ultimate Reality behind the ever-changing phenomenal world of things and beings. 'That Thou Art' (Tat Tvam Asi) is the teacher's advice. The student in his seat of meditation realises subjectively in himself that 'This Self within is Brahman' (Ayam Ātmā Brahma). Last comes the hallelujah that sings in the bosom of the now Liberated sage in the student and he in his sense of fulfilment and bliss immeasurable, confirms in a mad roar of joy and wonder, 'I am Brahman' (Ahaṁ Brahmāsmi).

Of these four Mahāvākyas, the statement containing the entire instruction of the teacher[1] is 'That Thou Art'. Therefore, this Mahāvākya of mere three words must have, in its mysterious depths, packed an endless array of precious suggestions and an unsuspected volume of magnificent imports. An ordinary student, with all his studies of the Upaniṣads, may not be able to handle, all by himself, this mantra efficiently and effectively in his seat of meditation, unless he is helped to open this treasure chamber, and is fully instructed how to enter and move amidst its fabulously rich, but confusingly laid out labyrinth of thought.

Exposition of this pithy but pregnant sentence (vākya), is accomplished by Ādi Śaṅkara in this lean-looking booklet of a mere 53 verses called *'Vākya vṛtti'*. Here we have an exhaustive exposition (vṛtti) of the great statement (vākya), 'That Thou Art'. The finite words that constitute the elementary blocks with which all languages are built, can never hope to express the Infinite, which is the theme of discussion in the subjective science of the Self (Brahmavidyā).

---

[1] *Chāndogya-upaniṣad* - dialogue between Sage Āruṇi and his son and disciple Śvetaketu.

Therefore, the ṛṣis and prophets had an unenviable job indeed – to express the inexpressible, to describe the indescribable, to explain that which is really inexplicable.

The Self is experienced on transcending the mind and intellect. Language is a vehicle for communication between intellects. Thus, words by themselves cannot fully express and efficiently communicate the knowledge of the supreme Self . This is an accepted fact to all ṛṣis and prophets around the world, who provided us with the scriptural knowledge from different parts of the world and at different periods of history.

Yet, it is a pleasant paradox that we find so many scriptures, each one of them a perfect masterpiece of literature, communicating the mystic experiences of the great Masters. Naturally, though the scriptures borrow and use the prevalent language of its age and the idiom popular at that time, in the area of its birth, yet, the words must have some subtle suggestive mystery about them on their own, if they were to describe the indescribable. Hence unique is the style of all the scriptures in the world.

To explain this underlying suggestiveness, which is never so readily obvious to an unprepared student, there must be a special study of the unique techniques employed in the sublime literature of the scriptures. This is very well brought out to the student's understanding in the prakriyā books. With the thoroughness of an artist, the precision of a scientist, the delightful delicacy of a flower opening in your courtyard all by itself, while nodding to the warm breeze in the springtime garden – Śaṅkara in his *Vākya vṛtti*, dissects the statement, 'Tat Tvaṃ Asi', and reveals its depth and significance to the student. The Mahāvākya clearly indicates that the Self in him is the Self everywhere, the Brahman.

The meaning of the words (vācyārtha) helps us to get at the meaning of the entire sentence (vākyārtha). The text that explains and demonstrates clearly the depth meaning (lakṣyārtha) of a pregnant and sacred scriptural statement is called *Vākya vṛtti.*

The quest in Vedānta is purely subjective. The seeker is searching to discover his own essential identity with the Self: who is he, who is expressing so constantly through his own body in all his worldly encounters? The world is the field of his play, the body is his 'toolkit' with which he contacts the fields of his experiences around him. Then, who is he, who is using his body and living his life of joys and sorrows, eked out from the world outside?

A searching intellect may come to feel that he is the mind. But his mind is also regulated, controlled and guided by his intellect. So then, can he be, in essence, his intellect? As we deeply ponder over it, is it not a fact that we are conscious of our own intellect and its endless dance of ideas? Therefore, the knower of the intellect must be the essential factor in me. This Consciousness that illumines the thoughts and emotions must be the ultimate Me in my own bosom.

This 'witnessing Consciousness' is 'Thou' in the Mahāvākya. The Reality – the changeless substratum supporting the universe of names and forms – the great grand ground upon which the world play is going on 'That' is Brahman. The Vaidika declaration, with surging conviction and doubtless courage asserts, 'That Thou Art', Brahman alone is your essential nature.

In order to make this declaration bless our individual life, each student needs some help: a kind of 'initiation'. The much abused term 'initiation' is dangerous as today it suggests to the common man some ritualistic fantasia, a convulsion of some 'cosmic' religious pageantry or a mysterious touch that accomplishes a staggering miracle by the teacher upon the student. These are all sheer poetic exaggerations, mere psychological props helpful, perhaps, to the emotional students, some powerful suggestions necessary, perhaps, to sentimental types.

The rational, alert and sharp intellects however understand 'initiation' as that by which the teacher guides the student's mind's entire attention to a more subtle, creative source in the student himself - beyond all perceivable, known fields including his own personal thoughts and emotions. This process of initiation is called meditation.

All these 53 verses are to be recognised as so many exercises in meditation – not merely verses to be studied and intellectually digested.

On awakening to this state of the Self within, the seeker realises the Brahman. Such a man, liberated in life, lives in an undisturbed state of peaceful recognition of his true identity with Brahman: sahaja samādhi. Never can the Self-realised one ever more come to live identified with his body-mind-intellect complex and play again the fool, as an individualised ego (jīva) in the world of things and beings.

The liberated-in-life (Jīvanmukta) certainly lives amidst us, as one of us, perceiving equally well our familiar world. Only he sees the world now, after realisation, in a new light, as an expression of the very Self in him. He cannot be any longer fascinated by the beautiful objects and the charming beings. Not that he runs away from the world, he lives and acts amidst us, not as a slave to the happenings, but as a saviour of the age and man.

He accepts everything, and he rejects nothing; he reflects everything, yet, keeps nothing, like a mirror!!

Swami Chinmayananda

TORONTO, (Canada),
8th August, 1981.

Introduction

As an inspired missionary, Ādi Śaṅkara could not rest content with merely producing exhaustive and splendid commentaries upon the Upaniṣads, the *Gītā* and the *Brahmasūtras*. He was anxious to communicate this knowledge to the children of the ṛṣis, the spiritual seekers of the world. In his infinite love, he conceived many textbooks to serve the need of the students at different levels of intellectual understanding on the subtle meaning of the texts and the techniques for the seekers' spiritual progress within. Here is a short, 53 verse text meant for students who have already cultivated in themselves the necessary inner purification to take off into contemplative flights.

Through devotion and dedicated service to the world around, when the inner psychological extrovertedness gets curbed, the mind gets surcharged with its own dynamism. Such an alert and quiet mind manifests its contemplative faculties, and to such a contemplative student Śaṅkara is prescribing the direction of his take-off.

The Upaniṣads have given out the four 'great statements' (the Mahāvākyas) and comtemplative students of Vedānta reach out to new dimensions of awareness through steady and intense contemplation upon the deep and inner significance of these intuitional statements. Of these four statements, in this textbook the discussion is on 'That Thou Art' ('Tat Tvam Asi').

Bhāṣya is a literature in which the Ācārya not only explains every word in the mantra (statements of the scriptures) but also explains his own words, inasmuch as he has to logically convince the students why he has interpreted words of the mantra as he has done.[1]

But to explain each word in the mantra as lucidly as the teacher can, is called a 'vṛtti'.[2] When these 'vṛttis' are again commented upon and brought out vividly to the total understanding of the student, at his level, the literature is called 'vārtikam.'[3]

---

[1] *sūtrārtho varṇyate yatra padaiḥ sūtrānusāribhiḥ.*
svapadāni ca varṇyante bhāṣyaṁ bhāṣyavido viduḥ.

[2] *sūtrasya arthavivaraṇam vṛttiḥ.*

[3] *vṛttiṁ vedayati iti vārtikam. (vṛtti vivaraṇam).*

Here is *Vākya vṛtti*. A book conceived and given out by Śaṅkara in the form of a dialogue where a student approaches a teacher, with a confession that the statement 'That Thou Art' does not add up to any vivid understanding in his mind. The teacher, with all love, is patiently elucidating what exactly the scripture means by the words employed in this significant sentence.

Mahāvākya came bursting forth from the intuitive great Masters out of their own direct experience of the one eternal, universal substratum, whose play is the world of names and forms, all experiences and happenings. Through contemplation and meditation, when the ṛṣi transcends his mind and gets awakened to the pure state of Brahman, and when such a teacher is approached by a student, seeking the knowledge of this Reality, in fact, there is no way in which the teacher can effectively communicate with the student. The Masters of the Upaniṣads and the teachers of Vedānta do successfully help the student through a special technique and hence the need for our surrender to our teacher, devotion to the Lord and the total obedience to the guidelines indicated by the teacher.

The first effort of the teacher is to make the student himself contemplative and when he has gained a contemplative mind, he becomes fit for this great initiation. When such a fit student approaches the teacher, the teacher clears his doubts and expands the theme, differently to different students, depending upon the student's background, his present state, his mental abilities and intellectual comprehension.

We have, in this short booklet, many hints given to indicate the qualities that the disciple should cultivate, which can help him to gain the right knowledge. The student enquires very minutely the significance of the words used and the teacher patiently, elaborately, almost exhaustively explains each word so that the statement contained in the sentence may become very clear to the contemplative seeker.

When the teachers use words in the scriptures, they are compelled to use words that have already gathered certain common significance, by the long usage of them in the society. He has to use those very same worn out words, but the student has to be lifted from the obvious meaning, and helped to recognise the deeper significances hinted at with these words, by the rich mind of the awakened Masters. Therefore, in this short book, Śaṅkara indicates how to reject the superficial meaning and reach at, through its significant suggestiveness, the voiceless state of the pure Essence behind the universe.

The poem concludes with a peroration for the purpose of emphasis, that the student should not ever overlook or give up diligent practice of virtues of self-control and repeated study of the scriptures until they come by themselves, to the firm and vivid understanding of the state described in the scriptures as 'I am Brahman' (Ahaṁ Brahmāsmi). The grace of the scriptures and the Masters can not only guide and lead us when we are confused but also support us en route when we are weary and tired, and remove all obstacles to make it a pleasant pilgrimage to the Higher, the timeless and therefore, changeless, birthless, deathless, undecaying, eternal, immortal, imperishable, and so on. A purified mind, at its seat of meditation, rides along these thoughts in the early states of contemplation and when mind gets soaked with these thoughts, it gathers greater meditative poise and in those moments of inner peace and knowledge the mind disappears into the vision - the infinite, non-dual Brahman.

An Exhaustive Explanation of the Statement 'That Thou Art' (Tat Tvam Asi).

Before undertaking any great work in the classical language, especially when the teachers deal with spiritual matters, it is not only a tradition but a necessity that they invoke the Lord and surrender themselves in devotion at His feet. To dehypnotise the mind from even vague traces of ego is to cleanse the mind totally, to let the Higher in the Master flow out to the seeker without being conditioned by the mind through which the message is gurgling out.

Here Śaṅkara starts the work *Vākya vṛtti* with the two opening verses, invoking in meditation the infinite Brahman and surrendering in devotion to the teacher and guide on the path.

सर्गस्थितिप्रलयहेतुमचिन्त्यशक्तिं
विश्वेश्वरं विदितविश्वमनन्तमूर्तिम्।
निर्मुक्तबन्धनमपारसुखाम्बुराशिं
श्रीवल्लभं विमलबोधघनं नमामि ॥१॥

sargasthitipralayahetumacintyaśaktiṁ
viśveśvaraṁ viditaviśvamanantamūrtim,
nirmuktabandhanamapārasukhāmburāśiṁ
śrīvallabhaṁ vimalabodhaghanaṁ namāmi. (1)

सर्गस्थितिप्रलयहेतुम् – the cause of creation, maintenance and dissolution (of the universe); अचिन्त्यशक्तिम् – inscrutable power; विश्वेश्वरम् – Lord of the universe; विदितविश्वम् – all knowing; अनन्तमूर्तिम् – having endless forms; निर्मुक्तबन्धनम् – ever free; अपारसुखाम्बुराशिम् – a shoreless ocean of happiness; श्रीवल्लभम् – the beloved of Lakṣmī (Śrī); विमलबोधघनम् – pure Consciousness Divine; नमामि – (I) bow down

1. I bow down to that pure Consciousness Divine – a shoreless ocean of happpiness, which is all-pervading (Viṣṇu), the beloved of Śrī, the all-knowing Lord of the universe, assuming endless forms yet ever free, having an inscrutable power to become (apparently) the cause of creation, maintenance and dissolution of the universe.

The state of pure Consciousness reveals itself to us when we transcend the limitations imposed upon ourselves due to our identification with our equipment of experiences. The body, mind and intellect are the only sources that spew out for us our endless sorrows, anxieties and disturbances. Thus, in terms of the student's own experiences, in his present state as a limited ego, the teachers of the Upaniṣads try to point out the supreme state, only as a 'shoreless ocean of happiness.'

Limitations of shape and form, incapacities and incapabilities with emotional and intellectual qualities are all suffered in the ego state alone; just as the walls of a pot appear to limit space into a temporary identity as 'pot space.' When the pot is broken, the pot space realises its total identity with the universal space. The Lord, the infinite Consciousness, His pure nature, is Viṣṇu, the all-pervading.

Being the substratum for the entire world of matter and its glories (Śrī), this limitless bliss state of pure Awareness is considered as the very enlivener of matter, the Lord of Śrī (Śrī Vallabha).

Just as a post appears to a deluded one as a person standing, a tree, a robber, a mugger or a ghost, yet the post has not changed at all. Just as millions of waves may arise, clash among themselves and disappear, yet no change has happened to the ocean deep in its depths – so too, all these endless varieties of names and forms that constitute the universe are all appearances of an apparent disturbance in the infinite Consciousness. The plurality of names and forms, their destinies of joys and sorrows, all clamourously happen in noisy confusion upon the changeless substratum, the pure Existence, is ever free from them all. The sufferings of a dreamer cannot affect its substratum, the waker's mind. Hence, Śaṅkara indicates the infinite Self, the Brahman, as assuming endless forms, yet ever free.

This divine Self in Its inscrutable power of deluding itself, comes to identify with the world of change and becomes thereby, God, the cause of creation, maintenance and dissolution. As in the microcosm, so in the macrocosm; in my mind I create my thoughts, I maintain them and I destroy them. The infinite Consciousness, identifying with the 'total mind and intellect' becomes thus, apparently the creator, sustainer and destroyer of the universe, the God, the cause of the universal play.

This delusory power is inherent in everyone of us. The non-apprehension of Reality compels the mind to project its own illusions, the hosts of its misapprehensions. Technically, in the science of Vedānta, this non-apprehension and its consequent misapprehensions are together called ignorance (avidyā) in the microcosm. In the macrocosm, this very same inscrutable power is indicated by the technical term 'māyā.' The Consciousness functioning through my avidyā becomes the sentient sense of individuality in me. The same infinite Consciousness functioning through māyā appears in our judgement as God, cause of the universe and its constant state of change.

The concept of the limited ego (jīva) and the concept of the Lord of the universe, God, are both superimposed upon the Brahman. I bow down to that pure Consciousness Divine.

यस्य प्रसादादहमेव विष्णु-
र्मय्येव सर्वं परिकल्पितं च
इत्थं विजानामि सदात्मरूपं
तस्याङ्घ्रिपद्मं प्रणतोऽस्मि नित्यम् ॥२॥

yasya prasādādahameva viṣṇur-
mayyeva sarvaṁ parikalpitaṁ ca
itthaṁ vijānāmi sadātmarūpaṁ
tasyāṅghripadmaṁ praṇato'smi nityam. (2)

यस्य – whose; प्रसादात् – by grace; अहम् – I; एव – alone; विष्णुः – all-pervading Essence; मयि – in me; एव – alone; सर्वम् – all; परिकल्पितम् – superimposed; च – and; इत्थम् – in this way; विजानामि – (I) realise; सदात्मरूपम् – world of multiplicity; तस्य – his; अङ्घ्रिपद्मम् – lotus feet; प्रणतः अस्मि – (I) prostrate; नित्यम् – always

2. *Again and again I prostrate at the feet of my Guru, by whose grace I have come to realise, 'I alone am the all pervading Essence (Viṣṇu)' and that 'the world of multiplicity is all a superimposition upon myself.'*

To tune our mind with the teacher is the only way to set ourselves for perfect communication with his words. After all, we have gone to the teacher to gain knowledge and arrive at wisdom. This subjective theme is not something that the teacher can transfer into our comprehension as in an objective science, because this is a state transcending the equipments – the body, mind and intellect. Through contemplation alone we gain the necessary poise in ourselves to glide away from our misconceptions and arrive at Self-knowledge.

I again and again prostrate, as not a mere repeated physical act of prostration, but a continuous (nityam) attitude of surrender to the teacher's instructions and guidance.

It is only through a process of perfect tuning-in that we come to experience a wave of refreshing sense of holiness and quietude in our otherwise disturbed and ugly bosom. The flooding in of this new sense of satisfaction and a cheerful indifference to everything else, creates a mood which is most conducive to creative listening and transformative contemplation. In this inner attitude, one's mind brings to expression new powers of comprehension and vision and the devoted student recognises them all as some inexplicable blessings arising from the grace of the teacher.

By the Guru's grace alone, the student arrives at his true knowledge culminating in the wisdom 'I alone am the all-pervading Essence, namely Viṣṇu.'

From this awakened state, the dream of plurality of things and beings and their dynamic actions are all recognised as something which was merely superimposed upon Me alone. In the non-apprehension of the true nature of a thing, the mind projects illusory visions and these delusory perceptions provide all our sorrows of existence.

I prostrate again and again to my teacher, by whose blessings alone I have come to awake to the state of Self, wherein I realise that the world as perceived by me in my ego state, was all illusory misconceptions of a restless intellect and a disturbed mind.

तापत्रयार्कसन्तप्तः कश्चिदुद्विग्नमानसः ।
शमादिसाधनैर्युक्तः सद्गुरुं परिपृच्छति ॥३ ॥

tāpatrayārkasantaptaḥ kaścidudvignamānasaḥ,
śamādisādhanairyuktaḥ sadgurum paripṛcchati. (3)

शिष्य उवाच

अनायासेन येनास्मान्मुच्येयं भवबन्धनात् ।
तन्मे संक्षिप्य भगवन्केवलं कृपया वद ॥४ ॥

śiṣya uvāca

anāyāsena yenāsmānmucyeyaṁ bhavabandhanāt,
tanme saṅkṣipya bhagavankevalaṁ kṛpayā vada. (4)

तापत्रयार्कसन्तप्तः – scorched by the blazing sun of the three types of miseries; कश्चित् – someone; उद्विग्नमानसः – with dejected mind; शमादिसाधनैः – with the means such as self-control etc.; युक्तः – endowed; सद्गुरुम् – noble teacher; परिपृच्छति – enquires

शिष्य उवाच – the disciple said; अनायासेन – without much effort; येन – by whose; अस्मात् – our; मुच्य – liberated;

इयम् – this; भवबन्धनात् – from sorrows of bondage; तत् – that; मे – to me; संक्षिप्य – briefly; भगवन् – O holy teacher; केवलम् – merely; कृपया – please; वद – tell

3. Scorched by the blazing sun of the three miseries, a student – dejected with the world and restless for release, having cultivated all the means of Liberation, especially such virtues as self-control and so on – enquires of a noble teacher.

The disciple said:

4. "Merely out of your grace and mercy, O holy teacher, please explain to me briefly the means by which I may easily get liberated from the sorrows of this bondage."

Every living being has to go unavoidably through endless miseries and they have all been classified under three heads: a) miseries arising from unknown sources (hand of God) are technically called as ādhidaivika; (b) miseries arising from known sources (world of things and beings), but over which I have no control now, in Vedānta are called as ādhibhautika; and (c) miseries that arise subjectively from my own body and mind are indicated in the scriptures as ādhyātmika.

The majority of us, in our frantic preoccupations with discovering temporary remedies for these, are often not even fully conscious of our own miseries. To feel defenceless against the scorching sun of the threefold miseries, is a deep and painful despair with the world around us. Then to reach such a state described as blissful, the student starts seeking the spiritual path that promises 'the end to all miseries – blissful state as described.' He cultivates in himself all the necessary qualities required for taming and disciplining his mind. Such a disciplined mind and intellect alone will have the ability to grasp the rich significance and deep suggestiveness in the mystic Master's crisp statements, to reflect upon them and to lift himself beyond the misty realms of his own mental confusions. With a quiet mind he contemplates upon the suggestive meaning of the pregnant 'great statements' and arrives at the goal indicated by the Masters of the Upaniṣads.

The qualities that would quieten the mind and help it to conserve its own entire vitality are prescribed in Vedānta as the four-fold qualifications (sādhana catuṣṭaya).

It is not only that the disciple must have all the necessary physical and mental qualities, but a true teacher also must have certain unavoidable accomplishments. He must be well-established in the higher Knowledge – the Self. It is not sufficient that he has the erudition and scholarship in the words of the texts of the scriptures. Therefore, Śaṅkara qualifies, a true teacher as 'a knower of Brahman' (Sadguru).

The knowledge of the 'Self' is the immediate means that helps the student to awake from all his confusions. Without the prescribed qualifications, Self-knowledge which is the theme of the Upaniṣads, which is the subject matter of the teacher's discussions, will not be received by the student in its right perspective and true significance.

When this knowledge is not complete and the student is not rich with the necessary qualifications, his own mental agitations become insurmountable obstacles on his path. Once these means of Liberation come, the path becomes clear and he feels 'I may easily get liberated from the bondage of world.'

To understand the meaning of the words of the great statements (Mahāvākyas[1]) and to dwell upon their deeper significance, is the most direct way to Self-knowledge, wherein the pilgrimage of the seeker is easy, pleasant and effortless (anāyāsena).

[1] The Mahāvākyas are four in number:

1) 'The Self, pure Consciousness is Brahman' (Prajñānam Brahma) – *Aitareya-upaniṣad;*
2) 'That Thou art', (Tat Tvam Asi) – *Chāndogya-upaniṣad;*
3) 'This Self is Brahman', (Ayam Ātmā Brahma) – *Māṇḍūkya-upaniṣad;*
4) 'I am Brahman' (Ahaṁ Brahmāsmi) – *Bṛhadāraṇyaka-upaniṣad.*

गुरुरुवाच

साध्वी ते वचनव्यक्तिः प्रतिभाति वदामि ते ।
इदं तदिति विस्पष्टं सावधानमनाः शृणु ॥५॥

gururuvāca

sādhvī te vacanavyaktiḥ pratibhāti vadāmi te,
idaṁ taditi vispaṣṭaṁ sāvadhānamanāḥ śṛṇu. (5)

गुरुः उवाच – the teacher said; साध्वी – excellent; ते – your; वचनव्यक्तिः – very clear; प्रतिभाति – expresses; वदामि – (I shall) tell; ते – to you; इदम् – this; तत् इदम् इति – That is this; विस्पष्टम् – vividly; सावधानमनाः – with a quiet and alert mind; शृणु – listen

The Teacher said :

5. "Your question is valid and so very clearly expressed. I shall answer it exhaustively to make as vivid to you as though you are seeing it near. Listen to me with a quiet and alert mind."

First Mahāvākya gives a definition of Brahman (lakṣaṇa vākya). Second Mahāvākya is the statement of advice (upadeśa vākya). The Third Mahāvākya is the direct experience of the student in his meditation seat (anubhava vākya). The last is the roar of realisation, echoed through the attitude in which he lives thereafter, 'I am Brahman' (prastāva vākya).

We are able to conceive a doubt and express it vividly only when we have given enough thought to it in our own mind. A vague suspicion of the possible presence of a misty doubt, somewhere at a distant corner of our mind, cannot be clearly captured in our thoughts, and therefore, we always fail to express them eloquently. Śaṅkara here is fully satisfied with the question, 'so very clearly expressed' that he characterises it as, 'your question is very valid.' From the standpoint of a man of greater erudition, the question may perhaps sound foolish, but to the student, at his present level of understanding, it is very valid and therefore, the teacher applauds and cries 'excellent' (sādhvī).

The teacher promises, 'I shall answer it exhaustively and vividly (vispaṣṭaṁ).' He promises that his description can bring the knowledge as vividly to the student as though 'you are seeing it near (Tat idaṁ iti).'

The nature of Reality, which is at this moment beyond comprehension and so appears to the student as something far away, hence the pronoun 'that' is used. When it becomes his own direct knowledge, it will seem very near, as the very being in the very student, 'nearer than the nearest' and hence, the pronoun 'this'. The teacher promises that if the student is faithful and ready to put forth the required effort diligently, the subtle knowledge of the Self can be brought into his immediate, direct experience as 'That is this' (Tat idaṁ iti).

In order to impart this subjective knowledge, since it is not an easy transfer of some clear information available in some textbook somewhere, nor is it an intellectual conclusion arrived at by the teacher, the communication of knowledge cannot be successful, unless the student himself directs his entire inner attention to the state of Self, which at best can only be indicated by the Teacher. Hence, the teacher implores, 'listen to me with a quiet and alert mind.'

Hearing is merely the physical function of the sense organ of audition. It is only when we bring what we hear to a quiet and alert mind, can we digest and assimilate what we have heard and turn our attention to the state of pure Being, which is indicated by the Master, as ever-present at the core of our own inner personality.

What exactly is this magical explanation, which is an inescapable sure means of Liberation, is now being indicated in the following verse.

तत्त्वमस्यादिवाक्योत्थं यज्जीवपरमात्मनोः ।
तादात्म्यविषयं ज्ञानं तदिदं मुक्तिसाधनम् ॥६ ॥

tattvamasyādivākyotthaṁ yajjīvaparamātmanoḥ,
tādātmyaviṣayaṁ jñānaṁ tadidaṁ muktisādhanam. (6)

तत्त्वमस्यादिवाक्योत्थम् – stemming forth from statements of Vedas such as 'That Thou Art'; **यज्जीवपरमात्मनोः** – that which is of the individual Self and the universal Self; **तादात्म्यविषयं ज्ञानम्** – knowledge of identity; **तत्** – that; **इदम्** – this; **मुक्तिसाधनम्** – means of Liberation

6. Direct knowledge of that total identity between the individual Self and the universal Self, stemming forth from the Vaidika statements such as 'That Thou Art' and so on, is the immediate means to Liberation.

That which triggers us to a new state of exploration into ourselves, which will uplift us from our present state of Consciousness to the very knowledge of the Self, is naturally, the most direct means of Liberation and to a life of total freedom from all the miseries that we suffer in the realm of change. Buffetted by the endless demands of our physical and mental equipments, stormed by the tides of problems provided by the challenging situations in the outer phenomenal world, over which we have no control, we come to feel desperately exhausted and experience that we are helpless slaves to life's happenings. Thereafter, to seek a freedom from this tight cocoon of sorrows becomes an imperative urgency to any intelligent seeker (mumukṣu).

The immediate means can only be direct knowledge, for it is the non-apprehension of Reality (ignorance) that breeds misapprehensions. The sorrows of saṁsāra arise out of our false identifications with the wrappings of matter around and about us.

The light of Consciousness, caught up in and playing through our physical, mental and intellectual equipments, functions as a sentient entity – the Perceiver-Feeler-Thinker I – and this egocentric sense of individuality is defined as the 'individualised Self' (jīvātmā). When an individual rediscovers that, in essence, the individualised Self, the ego in him, is nothing other than the universal Self (paramātmā), his ego ends and along with it, all his delusory sorrows must cease to be.

In order to arrive at this new dimension of understanding, we have to re-educate ourselves and realign our values. This is achieved in Vedānta by careful analysis of the words in the great Vaidika statements such as 'That Thou Art' and so on.

These statements are sparkling flashes of intuitive wisdom that flare up in the inspired words of the great Masters. They are mystic statements. Therefore, they speak more than what we hear, they mean more than what meets our ears.

This entire short booklet is an attempt of Śaṅkara to guide the comprehension of the student, through the mysterious and silent corridors of their suggestiveness into the vast, sunny courtyard of his own fuller understanding of his true identification with the real Self.

This rediscovery, arrived at through contemplation, undertaken by one's own well purified inner equipment, is the immediate means of Liberating oneself from all illusory, personal misconceptions.

शिष्य उवाच

को जीवः कः परश्चात्मा तादात्म्यं वा कथं तयोः।
तत्त्वमस्यादिवाक्यं वा कथं तत्प्रतिपादयेत् ॥७॥

śiṣya uvāca

ko jīvaḥ kaḥ paraścātmā tādātmyaṁ vā kathaṁ tayoḥ,
tattvamasyādivākyaṁ vā kathaṁ tatpratipādayet. (7)

शिष्यः उवाच – the disciple said; कः – who; जीवः – individual Self; कः – who; परः – the other; च – and; आत्मा – the Self; तादात्म्यम् – identity; वा – and; कथम् – how; तयोः – their; तत्त्वमस्यादिवाक्यम् – statements such as 'That Thou Art'; वा – and; कथम् – how; तत् – that; प्रतिपादयेत् – discuss and prove (elucidate)

The disciple said:

7. 'What is the individual Self? What, then is the universal Self? How can they both be identical? And, how can statements like 'That Thou Art' discuss and prove this identity?'

In all objective sciences, on hearing a statement made, if we know the language, to a large extent we shall understand what the speaker is talking about, especially when the speaker is well disciplined in his logical thinking processes and clear in his presentation. Here is a statement, 'That Thou Art.' The pronoun 'That' is often used for something far away and the word 'you' (Thou) is again a second person pronoun. How can the statement indicate any identity between two pronouns – one a second-person pronoun and another a third-person pronoun?

The statement when declared, I do hear, but it does not speak to me. How can such a statement discuss and prove, for my personal understanding, this identity?

The student is reading the statement and trying to grasp it through the dictionary meanings of the words employed. In our everyday worldly transactions, language is employed only for its superficial and direct meaning. This everyday language is being employed by the Masters to express their sublime mystical experience. This is achieved through the suggestiveness of these words. Such a unique usage of ordinary words, has given rise to the scriptural style, and the world's mystical literature.

An uninitiated student's confusion is totally valid and it is right that he should fail to grasp its full significance.

Hence, the teacher, in the following verse, in all sympathy, concurs with the student.

गुरुरुवाच

अत्र ब्रूमः समाधानं कोऽन्यो जीवस्त्वमेव हि।
यस्त्वं पृच्छसि मां कोऽहं ब्रह्मैवासि न संशयः ॥८ ॥

gururuvāca

atra brūmaḥ samādhānaṁ ko'nyo jīvastvameva hi,
yastvaṁ pṛcchasi māṁ ko'haṁ brahmaivāsi na saṁśayaḥ. (8)

गुरुः उवाच – the teacher said; अत्र – here (for this); ब्रूमः – (I) shall tell; समाधानम् – answer; कः – who; अन्यः – other; जीवः – individual Self; त्वम् – yourself; एव – alone; हि – indeed; यः – one who; त्वम् – you; पृच्छसि – ask; माम् – me; कः – who; अहम् – am I; ब्रह्म – Brahman / Truth; एव – alone; असि – are; न – no; संशयः – doubt

The teacher said:

8. I shall answer your question. Who else can be the individual Self (jīva) other than yourself, that asks me this question, 'Who am I?'. There is no doubt about it. You alone are Brahman.

Doubts in the mind of the student with their compelling urgency, can destroy in a flash all his inner poise and attention. It is an inner emergency situation. Help must reach him instantaneously. Therefore, the teacher immediately assures the student that there is a solution for this confusion in him, I shall answer your question. This assurance of the teacher, as though by a wave of a magic wand, compels the rising mental storm to subside and the student feels composed and comforted. To that attentive student, who has been thus comforted, the teacher announces the pure Truth, raw and unvarnished, which can, in some cases, ditch the student if he is not fully prepared into a greater embarrassing confusion!

Such shocks are repeatedly given to the students in Vedānta discipline to drive home to him that it is not purely an intellectual investigation. The student himself must be prepared to wing forth through contemplation, and arrive at his own awakening into this state indicated by the words of 'the great statements' (Mahāvākyas).

You yourself who expresses this doubt and asks me 'Who am I?' - in essence, you yourself are Brahman.

The doubt arose as a disturbance in your rational thinking. The Consciousness in you illumined this doubt, which you became conscious of, with your words, 'Who am I?' If this Consciousness were not there in you, you would not have been aware of the doubt and there would have been no doubter in you. This Consciousness in you that illumines your doubts is the one Consciousness which is in all bosoms, illumining their specific thought disturbances. Naturally, therefore the teacher, who is so well-rooted in this sense of identity with the supreme Consciousness, answers his disciple directly that the questioner himself is Brahman.

In his infinite devotion to the teacher and rooted in his firm faith in the Master, the student understands that even though the Truth has been revealed, he is not able to grasp its total import and therefore daringly continues his enquiry.

Other than you, who else can be the limited ego (jīva)? No one says that the body is me; everyone understands that this body is mine. True. Whose? The entity to whom they (the body, mind and intellect) belong is the limited ego personality in you, denoted by the first person singular, 'I'.

For the happiness of this ego each one exists and functions. The inert equipments, all by themselves, cannot feel the happiness. Who then in you experiences the happiness? It must be a sentient entity in yourself. That sentient one who is your own individual personality, must be the 'ego' in you and this alone is the jīva-factor at once, both the doer (kartā) and the enjoyer (bhoktā).

The inert equipments are many, but the sentient, vital presence should be the same in all equipments. The pure Self, caught up in the endless changes of moods and thoughts in your mind appears to be ever-changing and restless, the ego, limited and bound by its own thoughts.

This misapprehension arises out of the non-apprehension of your essential nature, as pure Awareness. When this ignorance is removed by the knowledge of the Self, all the misapprehensions of the miserable jīvahood ends and it awakes to realise its true, infinite nature as the one Self. From the unique standpoint of pure wisdom does the teacher assert that 'you, yourself are the Brahman.'

Let us say you are Mr. Babu, an intelligent and successful son of your father. When you are going for your marriage, you become a bridegroom. After marriage, a husband and as a husband, you cannot avoid being the son-in-law of her father, a brother-in-law of her brother, and yet, in and through all these relationships, you are nothing but Mr. Babu. The pure Consciousness functioning through the equipments (BMI), becomes the individual-Self (PFT). Even so, you are nothing but Brahman.

शिष्य उवाच

पदार्थमेव जानामि नाद्यापि भगवन्स्फुटम् ।
अहं ब्रह्मेति वाक्यार्थं प्रतिपद्ये कथं वद ॥९॥

śiṣya uvāca

padārthameva jānāmi nādyāpi bhagavansphuṭam,
ahaṁ brahmeti vākyārthaṁ pratipadye kathaṁ vada. (9)

शिष्यः उवाच - the disciple said; पदार्थम् – word meaning; एव – even; जानामि – (I) know; न – not; अद्य – now; अपि – also; भगवन् – O holy teacher; स्फुटम् – clearly; अहम् – I; ब्रह्म – Truth; इति – thus; वाक्यार्थम् – sentence meaning; प्रतिपद्ये – comprehend; कथम् – how; वद – tell

The disciple said:

9. Not even the word meaning do I fully grasp clearly; how can I then comprehend the significance of the sentence, 'I am Brahman?'

When I hear a simple sentence in a foreign language, I do not comprehend any sense in it, because the meaning of the words employed therein are dumb noises to me and do not convey any meaning at all.

Without sound, word is not possible, true. But sound without meaning is only some rattling noise. Only when sounds have an accepted meaning for two people can they become words. When such meaningful words are arranged in a grammatical sentence, they can fairly convey the idea the speaker is trying to communicate to the listeners.

When even the significance of the words used is not clear to me, how can I grasp the total import communicated by the sentence?

Holy Sir, you insist that the statement, 'That Thou art' can reveal the full knowledge of the Self and this contemplation upon its mystic suggestion is the immediate means for the ultimate spiritual experience, Self-knowledge. Certainly, I do hear the words of the great statement (Mahāvākya), but its words do not speak to me. Hence, I am not able to dwell upon the total identity of 'that' and 'Thou' as employed in the declaration.

Thus, when you say, in your infinite kindness 'I alone am Brahman' I honestly cannot comprehend the vast significance suggested by your simple statement. So please explain to me elaborately ,the words employed here.

The student is seeking more and more explanations in his attempt at a deeper enquiry in this dialogue between the teacher and the taught. The sympathetic teacher gets a glimpse of the quality of the student and accordingly, the teacher elaborates his explanations. A true teacher is never tired of helping his students.

गुरुरुवाच

सत्यमाह भवानत्र विगानं नैव विद्यते ।
हेतुः पदार्थबोधो हि वाक्यार्थावगतेरिह ॥१० ॥

gururuvāca

satyamāha bhavānatra vigānaṁ naiva vidyate,
hetuḥ padārthabodho hi vākyārthāvagateriha. (10)

गुरुः उवाच - the teacher said; सत्यम् – true; आह – said; भवान् – you; अत्र – here; विगानम् – no two opinions; न – not; एव – indeed; विद्यते – exists (employ); हेतुः – cause; पदार्थबोधः – meaning of the words; हि – surely; वाक्यार्थावगतेः – of the understanding of the sentence (containing those words); इह – in this matter

The teacher said:

10. You have said the truth when you complained that the knowledge and understanding of the meaning of the words employed in a sentence, are indeed the cause of the understanding of the full significance of the sentence. There are no two opinions about it.

The word meaning (padārtha) is the beginning stage of grasping the total significance of any complete statement (vākyārtha). Without the word meaning, no one can comprehend the significant idea indicated by the sentence; the word meanings alone can add up to the idea expressed in a statement. Thus, there is an intimate relationship between the exact meaning of the words employed and true import communicated by a total sentence under any study. There are no two opinions about it (vigānaṁ).

Again, the same word may often have different shades of meaning. The student has to reflect upon and decide correctly the exact shade of meaning, most suited in the context of the general thought development. Ascertaining intelligently the exact connotation in which the words are used by the author in a sentence is the secret of correctly arriving at the actual idea conveyed by the given sentence. For example, if the word 'bark' is used in a sentence, according to the context, the student must decide whether it is the bark of a tree or the bark of a dog. Else the true meaning of a sentence like, 'The bark at my window woke me up' cannot be intelligently interpreted. My dear child your complaint is true and nobody can contradict this (vigānaṁ).[1]

All these suggestions are implied in the disciple's demand for the exact meanings of the words employed in the great commandment, 'I am Brahman' (Ahaṁ Brahmāsmi).

The Teacher feels extremely gratified at the sincerity and alertness of the student, as revealed by the audacity and honesty in thus questioning the teacher. Such valid questions, when they come from the students, serve as windows through which the teacher peeps in and observes the subtle thinking processes in the intellect of the student. Once satisfied, the teacher starts his elaborate explanations for the specific words.

---

[1] The word Vigānam, also means 'contradiction.'

अन्तःकरणतद्वृत्तिसाक्षिचैतन्यविग्रहः ।
आनन्दरूपः सत्यः सन्किं नात्मानं प्रपद्यसे ॥११॥

antaḥkaraṇatadvṛttisākṣicaitanyavigrahaḥ,
ānandarūpaḥ satyaḥ sankiṁ nātmānaṁ prapadyase. (11)

अन्तःकरणतद्वृत्तिसाक्षिचैतन्यविग्रहः – the witnessing Light that illumines the inner equipment and their functions; आनन्दरूपः – of the nature of Bliss; सत्यः – Truth; सन् – being; किम् – why; न – not; आत्मानम् – your own Self; प्रपद्यसे – recognise

11. Why do you not recognise your own Self, which is an embodiment of eternal Bliss Essence, the witnessing Light that illumines the inner equipment and their functions?

From this verse onwards, through some sixteen verses,[1] the teacher explains the term 'Thou' in the great statement, 'That Thou Art.'

[1] Up to Verse 27.

The outer equipments of experience are the instruments of perceptions[1] and the instruments of action[2] and, as a contrast to these, Vedānta indicates the mind-intellect equipment in us, by the appellation, 'inner instruments[3].' All experiences in life are gained by the vigorous functioning of these subtle inner instruments through the grosser outer equipments. Therefore, we are apt to misunderstand that the individuality in us is the mind-intellect equipment, and, it is logical too. When they function, there is the individuality, and when they do not function, as in deep sleep or under chloroform, the individuality is absent in us. Therefore one can conclude that the complex of 'inner equipments' constitutes the sense of individuality in him.

Yet, if we subtly observe, we shall find that all the functions of the mind-intellect are awared by a subtler Essence in us. This Consciousness that illumines for us all the functions of our inner equipments, Itself remains as an uninvolved

[1] Eyes, ears, nose, tongue, and skin.

[2] Hands, feet, speech, genitals and the anus.

[3] Manas, buddhi, citta, ahaṅkāra – these four together is called the inner instruments, antaḥkaraṇa.

witness of all the modifications of the mind. The Consciousness thus, apparently caught in the web of our inner modifications, becomes our ego sense, the dynamic 'entity' in us. This individuality is in Vedānta known as the jīva - the ego in us.

The enjoyer (bhoktā) and the doer (kartā) are both the intellect and the mind is but an instrument of the intellect. In the play of the instruments of mind-intellect, the Witness that experiences them all is the essential 'Thou' in the statement, 'That Thou Art.'

An instrument is but a tool in accomplishing a job. In our personality, we have two sets of tools (karaṇam): the outer tools and the inner tools. The outer tools of perception are the grosser instruments through which we let in the outer sense objects to reach our mind, and the inner tools help us to gain our experience. The instruments of our response are the grosser equipments through which the mind manifests its responses.

But whose are these outer and inner equipments? In thoughtless hurry, we have concluded that we are the mind and intellect, the doer-enjoyer individual.

This ego is, in essence, the Consciousness, witnessing, illumining, knowing all the activities of both the outer and the inner equipments. That Witness alone can be you. This Witness is not only a mass of Consciousness, but also at once a state of pure Bliss. Even in our outer worldly sensuous pleasures, the sense objects only quieten our mind when the joy, which is the very nature of the Self, floods into our experience. When the stormy restlessness in a bosom, caused by its impatient desires, is suddenly calmed at the fulfilment of the desire, there is an explosive experience of Bliss. But again, that happiness is veiled by the rise of fresh waves of disturbance created by another set of desires.

Consciousness (caitanya) and Bliss (ānanda), are not two qualities (viśeṣa) of the Self. They are the very essence (dharma) of the Self; as light is of the fire, sweetness is of the sugar.

Apart from Consciousness (cit) and Bliss (ānanda) Self is also Existence Eternal (satya). That which remains the same, changeless in all the three periods of time – past, present and future, is called Satya, the Real. Our experiences change. Our equipments of experience – body, mind and intellect

– undergo modifications. The fields of experiences – objects, emotions and thoughts – keep on changing themselves. They, in their continuous dance among themselves, form and reform into endless patterns of situations and provide every living being with fresh challenges and new situations all the time. However, all along, the vital Consciousness, that illumines them all, is the same Truth, which is immutable and permanent – Satya.

Thus, the real Essence behind the 'Witness' the jīvātma, is the Self. This is indicated by the triple word idiom used here, 'Consciousness-Bliss-Truth' (caitanya-ānanda-satyam).[1] Here, these three are not three different aspects, but all of them indicate the one Essence which is expressed as Existence or as Knowledge or as Bliss in different equipments.

That which expresses as mere Existence (sat) in inert things (tāmasika), which again beams out as Knowledge (cit) among the dynamic mind-intellect functions (rājasika), is itself the one 'Self' which expresses as Bliss (ānanda), when the mind is quiet in its repose (sleep). To indicate that which expresses

[1] This is the famous triple word definition of the ṛṣis. 'Existence-Knowledge -Bliss' (Sat-Cit-Ānanda).

as Existence in the gross body, as Knowledge in the subtle body and as Bliss in the causal body, the ṛṣis had coined a word mixture, 'Sat-Cit-Ānanda' describing with these three indicative definitions Existence, Knowledge and Bliss, as the very spring of Consciousness in us, the Self.

This Self is the essential Being in you, and yet how is it that you are not able to experience it? Why do you not come to know your own Self? Is it so difficult? You are father to your children, husband to your wife and son to your father. Is it, then difficult for you to realise you, who is playing as the father, husband, and son?

Yet, it is difficult for the students to discover the Self. This can only be due to some long standing, mysterious inner confusion, a deep-seated, corroding self delusion, a tragic and blinding ignorance.

There must be a way to remove the confusion, to escape the delusion and to drive away the ignorance. That technique is now being pointed out by the teacher in the following verse.

सत्यानन्दस्वरूपं धीसाक्षिणं बोधविग्रहम् ।
चिन्तयात्मतया नित्यं त्यक्त्वा देहादिगां धियम् ॥१२ ॥

satyānandasvarūpaṁ dhīsākṣiṇaṁ bodhavigraham,
cintayātmatayā nityaṁ tyaktvā dehādigāṁ dhiyam. (12)

सत्यानन्दस्वरूपम् – of the nature of Existence Bliss; धीसाक्षिणम् – Witness of the intellect; बोधविग्रहम् – mass of pure Knowledge; चिन्तय – meditate; आत्मतया – as yourself; नित्यम् – always; त्यक्त्वा – giving up; देहादिगाम् – pertaining to body and so on; धियम् – misconception

12. Give up the intellectual misconception that the Self is the body and so on, and always meditate upon and think yourself to be the eternal Knowledge-Bliss – the Witness of the intellect – a sheer mass of pure Knowledge.

'As we think, so we become.' The present attitude of the mind and the values in the intellect are determined by the quality of our past thoughts. thought by thought, in the past, we have programmed our mind to behave as it does today in us. We think we are only the body-mind, we have, therefore, only such values that we respect which can bring our physical pleasure and material comforts. We have come to recognise ourselves as a limited ego, jīvātmā. Our vision of life becomes limited and naturally our values selfish and sensuous.

When this 'preoccupation with the not-Self' (anātma cintana) gets replaced by 'thoughts of the Self' (Ātma cintana), in time, the spiritual ignorance in the individual ends and the pure Self reveals Itself and is spiritually apprehended. Hence, the cry in all our scriptures for continued and regular meditation upon the Self.

Due to this ignorance of the real Self, our minds wander out, jogging from object to object in a frantic search for some satisfaction and sense of inner peace. Naturally, the mind gets extrovert and we get more and more steeped in the misapprehension that we are but the body-mind equipment in us. To ignore the Reality and to misapprehend it as the body is called body identification (deha adhyāsa). An aspirant for the spiritual awakening must end this false sense of his body identification, which is the perennial spring for all the sorrows and tragedies of a mortal in this finite world of things and beings.

So long as the ego fails to awake to its original state of pure Consciousness, the body identification cannot be totally wiped out. 'Body-I-am' is the natural experience in our present state of consciousness. A dreamer, so long as he is dreaming, cannot have even a vague notion of his own waker identity. He must awake to know, to discover, to realise, to experience his true identity as the waker.

In order to turn our minds' attention to the Self, some indications are given here. These indicative terms are together considered the 'definition' of the Self.

Existence-Knowledge-Bliss is the most dependable guidepost, pointing our attention to the Real and permanent in us – our true Being. This famous phrase, therefore, becomes its definition and when we learn to turn our total attention in this direction, that mind at that time, so held in all its devoted attention in this direction, is called a mind-at-meditation.

An intelligent man, observing himself and others, may readily come to conclude that the intellect is the Self because it is sentient, dynamic and our sole guide in all our actions. To fit the seeker's attention beyond the intellect, Śaṅkara here reminds us that the Self is but the illuminating 'witness of the intellect' (buddhi sākṣi). The activities of the rational intellect, their logical thinking processes, their conclusions and so on are all objects of our Consciousness. Thus, not only the outer world but even our own body, mind and intellect are objects of our Consciousness and therefore they all belong to the category of the not-Self. We are seeking the Self. The seeker is seeking his own Self, naturally he must gather all his wandering attention and turn it within to the spring of life in him, in full, wakeful alertness, to recognise this 'witness of the intellect.'

This Self is ever with us, yet to end our present misapprehension that we are the body – to end this body identification – long, continuous, sincere and devoted meditation upon the nature of the Self is needed. But how can the limited, finite and therefore ever-changing mind reach out to the infinite, changeless and permanent Self? It cannot. Mind at meditation turns away from all its preoccupations with the not-Self. Such a stilled mind, held in attention for the resurrecting experience of the Self, is mind at meditation.

The 'thought-flow' in an individual is his mind. When perceptions of the objective world have ceased, the ripples created by them in mind-stuff, called thoughts (vṛttis), must also cease. thoughtless mind is not a mind. In meditation, when the thoughts end, the mind disappears into the vision of the Real, the Self.

रूपादिमान्यतः पिण्डस्ततो नात्मा घटादिवत् ।
वियदादिमहाभूतविकारत्वाच्च कुम्भवत् ॥१३ ॥

rūpādimānyataḥ piṇḍastato nātmā ghaṭādivat,
viyadādimahābhūtavikāratvācca kumbhavat. (13)

रूपादिमान् – having form and so on; यतः – as; पिण्डः – the gross body; ततः – similarly; न – not; आत्मा – the Self; घटादिवत् – like pot and so on; वियदादिमहाभूतविकारत्वात् – due to being a modification of primal elements like space and so on; च – and; कुम्भवत् – like a pot

13. The body is not the Self, as like the pot, the body also has form. Again, the body is a modification of the great elements such as ākāśa, just like the pot.

From mud, pots are made, and mud is the material cause (upādāna kāraṇa) of the pots. Being eternal, the Self is not born; everything is being apparently born in the Self. Waves are born from, they exist in and ultimately perish into the ocean. The Self is not an effect, it is the cause of all effects. That which is immutable, is necessarily without birth and death, so it is never created or destroyed. The Self is spiritual (Ātmā), while the pot is material, and not Self (anātmā). The body is, like the pot, a product of the five great elements, essentially a product of matter. A body has birth, growth, decay and death; it is ever-changing and undergoes itself constant modifications. The body, like any piece of furniture, is a material object, belonging to the category of not-Self (Anātmā).

The dynamic activities of the body, its ability to know itself and its sense perceptions, are all expressions of Consciousness (Ātmā) through matter equipments, such as the sense organs of perceptions and actions, constituting the body.

The body grows and decays, it can grow fat or thin, therefore, it cannot be like a pot. This argument cannot be very true. A brick wall can grow as we continue building it and it can become shorter or thinner as we remove the bricks. The body grows with its powers of assimilation and when this is arrested by disease or old age, the growth also correspondingly ends. We cannot say that the growing brick wall is sentient. Thus, the body in itself is insentient, composed of mere matter, and it is anātmā.

Our gross body is an effect of our parents and also at once a cause for gross bodies of our children. The Self is neither a cause nor an effect. How then can the body be the Self? The gross body is made up of matter (anātmā), and the Self is the Spirit (Ātmā), pure Consciousness-Bliss. Naturally, the body, an 'object' of Consciousness, can never be the Self – the very Consciousness.

शिष्य उवाच

अनात्मा यदि पिण्डोऽयमुक्तहेतुबलान्मतः।
करामलकवत्साक्षादात्मानं प्रतिपादय ॥१४॥

siśya uvāca

anātmā yadi piṇḍo'yamuktahetubalānmataḥ,
karāmalakavatsākṣādātmānaṁ pratipādaya. (14)

शिष्य उवाच – the disciple said; अनात्मा – not-Self; यदि – if; पिण्डः – gross body; अयम् – this; उक्तहेतुबलात् – by the strength of mentioned reasons; मतः – considered; करामलकवत् – as a fruit in hand; साक्षात् – directly; आत्मानम् – the Self; प्रतिपादय – explain.

The disciple said:

14. If, by the strength of these arguments, the gross body is considered as 'not-Self' then please explain exhaustively and directly indicate the Self – as clearly as a fruit in hand.

Drawing a conclusion from given premises is called inference[1]. Here, the Guru is employing an inference to prove that the gross body is not-Self. Like a pot, the body is made up of elements, so the body also is not-Self. Here 'body' is pakṣa, 'not-Self' is sādhya, 'because it is made up of the five elements' is the hetu and the 'pot' is the dṛṣṭānta. The pot, made up of the great elements, is matter, so too the body, being made up of matter, must also be not-Self (anātmā). The hetu is powerful enough that the disciple admits that the inference compels him to accept the conclusion inferred, that the body is not-Self.

To recognise the not-Self status of the body may perhaps be a stage in the seeking, but the essential experience demanded by the seeker is of the Self. Thus, the student demands from the teacher an exhaustive and clear discourse by which the seeking heart may be fully satisfied with the experience of the nature of the Self.

The direct experience of the Self cannot be until it becomes available as readily as a fruit in hand. By

[1] Inference is termed in Sanskrit as anumāna. It has generally four aspects in it: 'sādhya' the proposition to be inferred; 'pakṣa' the subject or that in which the thing is inferred; 'hetu' the reason or ground of inference and dṛṣṭānta, the illustration.

hinting and even by proving that the body is not the Self, the teacher has negatively pointed out, by suggestion, the existence of Self. This appears to be unsatisfactory and totally insufficient to quench the seeker's enthusiasm. The disciple is insisting that he should gain a direct knowledge of the Self.

If the body is not the Self, how am I to end my body sense? If I, in a rash act, annihilate the body, who will perceive the Ātman which may survive the annihilation of the anātman? If you say that the body need not be destroyed, and that we have only to end our body identification, please indicate to me the means for achieving this state. Also, give me a hint as to how I can then experience this great, grand state which appears to be, at best, a hypothetical possibility. Let me have this knowledge, please, as readily for my examination and total apprehension as a plum fruit, right in my palm.

If such a direct experience of the Self is not possible, explain to me what other means of knowledge I should pursue to gain a close, intimate and total experience of the Self.

गुरुरुवाच

घटद्रष्टा घटाद्भिन्नः सर्वथा न घटो यथा ।
देहद्रष्टा तथा देहो नाहमित्यवधारय ॥१५॥

gururuvāca

ghaṭadraṣṭā ghaṭādbhinnaḥ sarvathā na ghaṭo yathā,
dehadraṣṭā tathā deho nāhamityavadhāraya. (15)

गुरुः उवाच : – the teacher said: घटद्रष्टा – perceiver of a pot; घटात् – from the pot; भिन्नः – different; सर्वथा – ever; न – not; घटः – pot; यथा – just as; देहद्रष्टा – perceiver of the body; तथा – so too; देहः – body; न – not; अहम् – I; इति – thus; अवधारय – ascertain

The teacher said:

15. Just as the perceiver of a pot is ever distinctly different from the pot and can never be the pot, so too, you, the perceiver of your body, are distinct from your body and can never be the body. This you firmly ascertain in yourself.

The demand of the student was to gain a direct experience of the Self in him. A direct experience means: an individual, as a subject, experiences a given object through his sense organs and the mind. Such a subject-object relationship cannot remain in the One, infinite Self. Therefore, direct experience of the Self is not through the sense organs or mind or intellect (nor a combination of them all); the Self transcends them all.

The teacher has to indicate that the only means available is through contemplation. But the student, at this stage, cannot appreciate, nor even understand it.

The teacher has to, very persuasively, guide the seeker, through logical arguments and set him firmly on the path of contemplation. This is a delicate operation and the gracious teacher, with his loving sensitivity, accomplishes this miracle or transformation of intellectual thinking into an easy, effortless contemplative gliding.

The Teacher steadily lifts the student's perception away from the matter equipments and turns him on to be within himself in a steady contemplative poise.

When you see an object, certainly you, the seer, are always distinctly different from the object seen. Your body is perceived by you; it is the seen.

Therefore, you, the seer of your body, are certainly separate from the body. Let us first of all ascertain this well in our understanding. Again, we claim that the body is ours. In fact, one can never be what one owns. The body is the possessed and you are the possessor. I cannot be my dog; the dog belongs to me; I am its owner – the sole proprietor of my dog. Thus, the body is not you although the body is yours. You are something other than the body, who is the owner, proprietor and master of the body. Again and again assert this truth, come to change your attitude towards your body and re-establish your right relationship to the world of objects contacted and experienced through the body.

When, by this process, the body identification ceases to be, the spiritual ignorance (avidyā) to that extent gets eliminated. 'I am the body' idea is a peculiar stink that rises from the foul ditch of our spiritual ignorance. This false sense ushers in all the storms of thoughts – passions, worries, anxieties, fears, joys, sorrows – into man's mind. This noisy state of the choppy mind in surge, is that which veils the splendour and bliss of the Self from one's direct experience.

एवमिन्द्रियदृङ्नाहमिन्द्रियाणीती निश्चिनु ।
मनोबुद्धिस्तथा प्राणो नाहमित्यवधारय ॥१६ ॥

evamindriyadṛṅnāhamindriyāṇītī niścinu,
manobuddhistathā prāṇo nāhamityavadhāraya. (16)

एवम् – similarly; **इन्द्रियदृक्** – the seer of senses; **न** – not; **अहम्** – I; **इन्द्रियाणि** – senses; **इति** – thus; **निश्चिनु** – be sure; **मनोबुद्धिः** – mind and intellect; **तथा** – similarly; **प्राणः** – vital air; **न** – not; **अहम्** – I; **इति** – thus; **अवधारय** – ascertain

16. Similarly, be sure in yourself that you, the seer of the senses, are not the senses themselves. Ascertain that you are neither the mind, nor the intellect, nor the vital air (prāṇa).

After explaining to the student that he is not the gross body, in this verse, he is made to understand that he cannot be the subtle body also. The sense faculties of perceptions and actions (indriyas), vital air (prāṇa), mind and intellect together constitute the subtle body and without them, the outer gross sense organs and the body cannot function. This subtle body is also made up of the subtle aspects of the five great elements, and as such, it also falls under the categories of matter (anātmā).

Again, that we have sense faculties, prāṇa, mind, intellect and so on, is constantly known by us as we are conscious of them and their functions. The knower can never be the known.

We can 'see' the condition of our prāṇa, the nature of our mind and the state of our intellect. The one who sees the subtle body, becomes aware of its changing moods and evaluates the qualities of its performances, must necessarily be someone other than the subtle body. The advice to the student of Vedānta is that he, through independent analysis and careful arguments, must teach himself to gain a growing conviction in himself that he is the 'seer' of his subtle body. Surely, therefore he is something other than the subtle body because the 'seer' cannot be the seen.

Ascertain, 'I am the Lord of the sense organs, prāṇa, mind, intellect and so on. I take work out of them. I am not myself the subtle body, but I am the knower of the nature and quality of performance of the various limbs of my subtle body.'

The subtle body, like the sense organs and the limbs of the gross body, is an instrument, a tool kit. A workman accomplishes his job with the instruments; no job is done by the tools. Similarly, sense organs, their faculties, mind, intellect and so on, are all my outer and inner tools (karaṇa), and I who wield them in shaping the experiences of my life, can be but someone other than the tools. Only when the mind is available can the sense organs function. When the mind receives sense stimuli through the sense organs, it is known by the discriminative intellect. The intellect's judgement upon them and the exact responses they have ordered are also again known by me. Thus, I, who am the 'knower' of the intellect, must necessarily be something other than the intellect and all other instruments that have helped the intellect to come to its moment to moment judgements.

Breathing in and out is one of the gross and explicit manifestations of the prāṇa. This vital force (prāṇa) expresses in us as the various physiological functions. These activities are only an expression of the dynamism (rajoguṇa aspect) of all the five great elements. Prāṇa is also, therefore, in itself an expression of matter (anātmā) and not the Self (Ātmā).

Thus, firmly ascertain in yourself that you are something other than the gross and the subtle bodies.

सङ्घातोऽपि तथा नाहमिति दृश्यविलक्षणम् ।
द्रष्टारमनुमानेन निपुणं सम्प्रधारय ॥१७ ॥

saṅghāto'pi tathā nāhamiti dṛśyavilakṣaṇam,
draṣṭāramanumānena nipuṇaṁ sampradhāraya. (17)

सङ्घातः – the association (of gross and subtle bodies); **अपि** – also; **तथा** – similarly; **न** – not; **अहम्** – I; **इति** – thus; **दृश्यविलक्षणम्** – distinct from the seen; **द्रष्टारम्** – the seer; **अनुमानेन** – by inference; **निपुणम्** – intelligently; **सम्प्रधारय** – be sure (ascertain)

17. Similarly be sure that you are not the complex of the gross and the subtle bodies. Intelligently determine by inference, that you, the 'seer' are entirely distinct from the 'seen'.

If this gross body, with its sense organs of perception and action and the subtle body, with its mind and intellect, are not the Self, maybe the Ātman is a combination of all these, functioning at once as a complex (saṅghāta). Even though each of them has been already analysed and found as belonging to the realm of matter (anātmā), together when they function, they may be producing this new aspect,[1] recognised as the Consciousness. For example: each thread or fibre may have no strength, but when many of them are spun together and twisted into a rope, it can gain formidable strength and an admirable efficiency which were not there in the initial fibre or thread. The teacher here clearly indicates that the complex of the gross and subtle bodies also cannot be Self. Each fibre or thread has certainly some strength, and the great strength of the rope or the cord is but the sum total strength of the individual fibres that have gone into its make-up. In that twisting, the concerted strength of all the fibres is brought to express with a singular harmony, hence the strength of the rope. It is not something totally new that has come to manifest itself in the rope. The unborn and therefore, the undying 'Self' cannot be the product of the complex (saṅghāta).

This should be intelligently inferred. Here the inference is to be the complex of the bodies, gross

[1] Pāna – leaf, nuts and lime together when they are chewed, a property which was not in anyone of them, the red colour, rises. Similarly, maybe Consciousness happens in the saṅghāta.

and subtle, being seen, cannot be the seer. The seen is ever distinctly different from the seer as a pot seen is different from the seer of the pot. Thus, with your discriminative intellect, very intelligently ascertain in yourself that the gross subtle complex in you also is but the not-Self (anātmā).

Here, the student can protest that he pointedly asked of the teacher to explain to him, to his full satisfaction, the nature of the Self. But the teacher has been discussing all along, elaborately the gross and subtle bodies and their complex, only to conclude at the end that they all together constitute the not-Self (anātmā). Why confuse me and waste my time by explaining so exhaustively the realm of matter (anātmā) when our discussion is precisely upon the Self (Ātman)? The misapprehension that the products of matter, such as body, mind and intellect, are the Self, is an experience caused by the non-apprehension of the spiritual Essence. In short the non-apprehension of the supreme Self in all its supreme transcendental resplendency, generates endless misapprehensions. To remove this non-apprehension, the spiritual ignorance (avidyā), is to invoke the Knowledge, the direct apprehension of the Self.

The sick regains his health when the cause for disease (the germ), is destroyed. The unveiling is a simple act which reveals the pictures behind the veiling. When our mental misapprehensions are quietened and eliminated, we should become fit for the direct apprehension of the Self. Hence, our attention is brought to focus intensively to observe, analyse, and logically re-evaluate our present misapprehensions. When the seeker realises that his gross and subtle bodies and their complex, are indeed the not-Self (anātmā), he is made to drop his sad, miserable, tragic and helpless identifications with them.

The dreamer, on ending his dream identification, awakes to realise that he is but himself the waker. So too, when the identifications of the not-Self end, 'Self-am-I' is experienced, 'there is no other way' scream the Upaniṣads.

देहेन्द्रियादयो भावा हानादिव्यापृतिक्षमाः ।
यस्य सन्निधिमात्रेण सोऽहमित्यवधारय ॥१८ ॥

dehendriyādayo bhāvā hānādivyāpṛtikṣamāḥ,
yasya sannidhimātreṇa so'hamityavadhāraya. (18)

देहेन्द्रियादयः – the body and the senses; भावाः – entities; हानादिव्यापृतिक्षमाः – capable of acceptance and rejection; यस्य – whose; सन्निधिमात्रेण – due to presence alone; सः – He; अहम् – I; इति – thus; अवधारय – ascertain

18. Thus ascertain, 'I am He' – the One because of whose presence alone the inert entities like the body and the senses, are able to function through acceptance and rejection.

So far, the realm of the not-Self was described and clearly brought to the easy comprehension of the student. Now the teacher starts explaining what the scriptures mean by the term 'Ātman' (Self). Matter (anātmā) is ever inert. Yet, the matter equipments, like the body, mind and intellect, are constantly working and dynamically functioning in all activities so long as the individual is alive. At the same time, we cannot say that the Self functions through matter – as the Self is a non-doer (akartā).

Again, both the Self and the not-Self cannot exist together in any plane. Matter exists only in the present plane of our egocentric consciousness, while Spirit, the Self, alone exists when we are in that transcendental plane of God-consciousness. The only acceptable theory, therefore would be that matter, though inert, comes to manifest its dynamism only in the presence of the Self.

Just as the world of beings (plant, animal and human) draws all its energy from the sun and yet each is free to act according to its own inclinations, so too in the presence of the supreme Consciousness, the body, mind, and intellect get charged with sentiency and dynamism. They have thereafter, total freedom to act as they like fulfilling the available vāsanās in the individual. The anātmā realm seems to bask in the spiritual presence of the Self and enlivened by this majestic presence, matter equipments dash out to strive to function and to achieve, each in their own respective fields.

Remember, all explanations are always for the ignorant, to help him end his non-apprehension of

Truth and therefore end all consequent false misapprehensions. Even the intellect is inert, but in the proximity of the Self it gets activated. This is an explanation addressed to one who is now suffering from his non-apprehension of the spiritual Essence. In the final experience of the one eternal Self, there is no existence of the not-Self for the Self to enliven.

When the sense organs, mind and intellect are thus geared to their respective performances by the mere grace or presence of the Self, then they frisk about and scream in joy; receiving sense stimuli from the sense objects, and expressing their responses in the world of activities. In this perception-response (grahaṇa-tyāga) activity of life, the outer sense organs of preception become the receiving equipments, and the organs of action serve as the instruments of all our responses – rejection–equipments (responses).

In all these activities of the mind and body, the Self is uninvolved. It by mere presence, enlivens everything. Realise intimately this Self, in a total and complete identification with It, as 'He am I' (So'ham).

From this verse (18) onwards, the following eight verses can be considered as helpful suggestions to assert our true Being in our seat of contemplation.

अनापन्नविकारः सन्नयस्कान्तवदेव यः।
बुद्ध्यादींश्चालयेत्प्रत्यक् सोऽहमित्यवधारय ॥१९॥

anāpannavikāraḥ sannayaskāntavadeva yaḥ,
buddhyādīṁścālayetpratyak so'hamityavadhāraya. (19)

अनापत् अविकारः सन् – being innermost and changeless; अयस्कान्तवत् एव – like a magnet and iron (magnet attracting iron); यः – who; बुद्ध्यादीन् – the intellect and so on; चालयेत् – moves; प्रत्यक् – innermost; सः अहम् – He I am; इति – thus; अवधारय – ascertain

19. Thus ascertain, He I am, the one changeless innermost Self that moves the intellect and so on, as a magnet does the iron filings.

When we say that in the presence of the Self the intellect, mind and sense organs act, we are apt to suspect whether some corresponding changes are also taking place in the Self, as it sounds as though the Self is apparently involved in these activities, or at least active, perhaps, in enlivening the anātmā. No modification is ever possible in the changeless (nirvikāra) Self. In fact, the reflected sun may appear to get shattered when the water surface is disturbed, but surely the sun is not affected by the shimmering disaster suffered by the reflected sun. In the worldly point of view, when electricity in its presence, lends to the bulb its incandescence; when gasoline releases the horsepower of the engine, the energy itself gets consumed in performing the work. Similarly, the student wonders if the Self is getting consumed as the equipments are enlivened.

To sweep out any such lingering doubts in the minds of the students, Śaṅkara smartly employs this verse. The Self is changeless (nirvikāra). Yet, in Its mere presence, the intellect and so on, get enlivened to activity. They do act always according to their own natural inclinations. This is, insists the teacher, 'something like the play of the iron filings in the mere presence of a magnet' (aya-skānta). The magnet is in no way affected, although the iron filings are visibly made to behave in a given pattern .

Understand and come to live that you are asserting this inner Self, in whose very presence alone the body-mind-intellect equipment functions as though sentient and alive. He who by His mere presence, enlivens everything, without Himself ever undergoing any change – 'He am I' (So'ham).

अजडात्मवदाभान्ति यत्सान्निध्याज्जडा अपि ।
देहेन्द्रियमनः प्राणाः सोऽहमित्यवधारय ॥२० ॥

ajaḍātmavadābhānti yatsānnidhyājjaḍā api,
dehendriyamanaḥ prāṇāḥ so'hamityavadhāraya. (20)

अजडात्मवत् आभान्ति – appear to be conscious and dynamic; यत्सान्निध्यात् – in whose presence; जडाः – inert; अपि – though; देहेन्द्रियमनःप्राणाः – the body, senses, mind, and vital air; सः अहम् – He I am; इति – thus; अवधारय – ascertain

20. Thus ascertain, He I am, the One Entity in whose vital presence the body, senses, mind and prāṇas, though inert in themselves, appear to be conscious and dynamic, as though they are the Self.

The body and other equipments are indeed by themselves inert and insentient. They are all made up of gross and subtle matter and matter is ever inert and insentient. But, they appear to be dynamic and conscious only when they are in the illusory presence of the Self – illusory because in the Self there is no play of matter; in It, nothing else exists. It is full[1]'(pūrṇam).

That the body is inert is seen when it is in sleep or under chloroform, swooning or dead. The dead body is as inert as a stone. Not only is the body thus, in its true nature inert, but so too are the mind-intellect-prāṇa and so on. All of them are constantly undergoing modifications, and those that undergo change (vikārī), are matter – conditioned by time, the anātmā; and matter is inert.

No doubt, the 'Self' cannot be perceived directly by your equipments of knowledge; it is not an 'object' of knowledge – it is the very 'subject'. But, through inference, we can come to comprehend the existence of the 'Self' as the very spring of all Consciousness, under the grace of which all inert equipment act and function as though fully sentient.

1 Undifferentiated Essence in which there are no distinctions in itself (svagata), within the species (sajātīya), or with other species (vijātīya) is called full (pūrṇam). For example, a black goat is different from other goats of different colours within the same species, and the goat is different from the cow of another species, and within the goat, the head is not like the legs, the legs are not like its tail. A thing that has no such distinctions in itself or with reference to others, is called pūrṇam.

When the mind is not in contact with them, the sense organs are helpless and inert. Mind itself is inert, it has light only when Self (light) reflects on it. The moon is lit up only by the light of the sun and thereafter the moonlight can illumine the mountains, dales, meadows and valleys stretched and shimmering under its soft light. Thus, the light of the Self, reflected in the mind-intellect equipment (cidābhāsa), is that which lends intelligence to the perceiving sense organs.

This subtle source of all Consciousness, the Self, is your real nature. Assert again and again, come to realise 'He am I' (So'ham).

अगमन्मे मनोऽन्यत्र साम्प्रतं च स्थिरीकृतम्।
एवं यो वेत्ति धीवृत्तिं सोऽहमित्यवधारय ॥ २१ ॥

agamanme mano'nyatra sāmpratam̐ ca sthirīkṛtam,
evam̐ yo vetti dhīvṛttim̐ so'hamityavadhāraya. (21)

अगमत् – went; मे – my; मनः – mind; अन्यत्र – elsewhere; साम्प्रतम् – now; च – and; स्थिरीकृतम् –has been brought to rest; एवम् – in this way; यः – who (the one); वेत्ति – knows; धीवृत्तिम् – modifications in mind; सः अहम् – He I am; इति – thus; अवधारय – ascertain

21. Thus ascertain, 'He am I', the one Consciousness, which is the Self that illumines the modifications in my mind such as 'my mind went elsewhere, however it has been brought to rest now.'

We had already explained that the sense organs cannot function without the mind and the mind is the factor that experiences the sense stimuli brought in by the sense organs. The intellect in us is the discriminative faculty that knows and judges the mind and all its activities. Till now, my mind was engaged in the thoughts of such an object. Now it has left that object, become peaceful and concentrated in meditation,' are all discriminated and known by my intellect.

Thus here the intellect is the seer and the mind is the seen – no doubt, these are all extremely relative. Intellect itself is made up of matter (anātmā) and so it has no sentiency of its own. The light of Consciousness playing in the intellect, becomes the intelligence and intellect becomes conscious enough to judge and know the condition of restlessness or quietude of the mind at any given time.

Mind and intellect are the two aspects of the same inner equipment (antaḥkaraṇa), the subtle body. But, just as you can watch your own leg or hands moving, just as a dog can lie down rolled upon itself on the sitting room carpet and watch its own tail moving, similarly, the Consciousness soaked intellect (cidābhāsa) knows the fluctuations and vagaries of the mind.

In its extrovertednesss, my mind prompted by its own inherent desires, roamed about among the sense objects and got itself excited and agitated. Now, in my meditation seat, my mind has temporarily left its fields of objects and has become relatively quiet. Such an experience can come to every seeker. One who knows this and therefore is the knower of one's own mental conditions, must be something other than the mind and intellect equipment.

Certainly, the inert intellect, which is itself an aspect of the subtle body, cannot be the final Self. Assert again and again, discover and come to realise, 'He am I' (So'ham).

Just as the sense organs are the knower of the sense objects, the mind is the knower of the senses and the intellect is the knower of the mind. Then, who is the illuminator of the intellect? This is brought out very clearly in the following verse.

स्वप्नजागरिते सुप्ति भावाभावौ धियां तथा ।
यो वेत्त्यविक्रियः साक्षात्सोऽहमित्यवधारय ॥२२ ॥

svapnajāgarite supti bhāvābhāvau dhiyāṁ tathā,
yo vettyavikriyaḥ sākṣātso'hamityavadhāraya. (22)

स्वप्नजागरिते – states of waking and dream; सुप्ति – deep sleep; भावाभावौ – appearance and disappearance; धियाम् – of the intellect; तथा – and also; यः – who; वेत्ति – knows; अविक्रियः – changeless; साक्षात् – directly cognised; सः अहम् – He am I; इति – thus; अवधारय – ascertain

22. He am I, the one Consciousness which is the changeless Self that is directly cognised, that illumines the three states of waking, dream and deep sleep; and that which illumines appearance and disappearance of the intellect and its functions – 'He am I' (So'ham) – ascertain thus and realise.

Intellect is ever-changing; therefore, it is limited. Since it is a limited equipment, its knowledge can be limited. The one whose ability to know is limited and conditioned, cannot be pure Knowledge which is glorified in the scriptures as unlimited, unconditioned, infinite, the Self.

The one Consciousness in us illumines all experiences (bhāva) in our waking, dream, and deep sleep states. The play of Consciousness is unbroken and continuous. All experiences, in the waking and dream states and also 'the absence of experiences' in the deep sleep state are illumined by the one light of Consciousness in us.

This seat of the ever bright, ever shining Consciousness, is the Self. It is in the presence of this Self that one 'knows' the appearance of thoughts in the waking and dream states and the disappearance of thoughts in sleep, swooning and so on, in the intellect. 'He am I' (So'ham).

Just as the light of a lamp is not affected by what it illumines, so too the Consciousness, the Self, is never affected by the fluctuations of the intellect, roamings of the mind, or by the tireless wanderings of the senses. The one Self illumines all the activities of all equipments, in every living being, all through their waking and dream states. The same Self illumines the 'disappearance' of all perceptions, in all intellects, in the deep sleep state. This one changeless (nirvikāra) mass of Consciousness, the 'Self' am I (So'ham) – thus, sincerely assert and come to realise it.

घटावभासको दीपो घटादन्यो यथेष्यते ।
देहावभासको देही तथाहं बोधविग्रहः ॥२३ ॥

ghaṭāvabhāsako dīpo ghaṭādanyo yatheṣyate,
dehāvabhāsako dehī tathāhaṁ bodhavigrahaḥ. (23)

घटावभासकः – illuminator of a pot; दीपः – lamp; घटात् – from the pot; अन्यः – different; यथा – just as; इष्यते – considered; देहावभासकः – the illuminator of the body; देही – the Self; तथा – so; अहम् – I; बोधविग्रहः – mass of Consciousness

23. Know yourself to be the one Self – a homogenous mass of Consciousness, which is the illuminator of the body and therefore quite distinct from it; just as a lamp that illumines a pot is always different from the pot illumined. I am a mass of Consciousness (Ahaṁ bodhavigrahaḥ).

The one constant Awareness in us makes us conscious of all our equipment of experiences the body-mind-intellect and also their respective fields of experiences – objects-emotions-thoughts. Illuminator is ever distinct from the illumined. The joys and sorrows of the equipment, their limitations and destinies cannot affect the Self in the least. The light of the lamp is never affected by the objects (pots) it illumines.

This 'Self' (Ātman) is the same in all creatures it is ever-present everywhere in its all-pervasive infinitude, illuminating at once all perceptions, feelings and thoughts in all sentient creatures. Hence, He is omniscient. This mass of Consciousness (bodhavigrahaḥ) 'the 'Self' am I.' Thus assert and realise Truth as your own essential nature. Wake up into the spiritual plane; end the sorrows of the limited and of the imperfect world of plurality, which is but the delusory experience of the ego, the jīvātmā.

In fact, jīva itself is nothing but the Self seen through the body-mind-intellect and their activities. The supreme infinite Consciousness functioning upon the complex of matter, the agitations of the mind and intellect, veil the true nature of the Self and It appears to be the sorrow-ridden, limited, miserable ego – jīva. End this non-apprehension of the 'Self' by asserting and realising your true nature as the pure changeless Consciousness (bodhavigrahaḥ).

पुत्रवित्तादयो भावा यस्य शेषतया प्रियाः ।
द्रष्टा सर्वप्रियतमः सोऽहमित्यवधारय ॥२४ ॥

putravittādayo bhāvā yasya śeṣatayā priyāḥ,
draṣṭā sarvapriyatamaḥ so'hamityavadhāraya. (24)

पुत्रवित्तादयः भावाः – beings and things such as children and wealth and so on; यस्य शेषतया – the one for whose sake; प्रियाः – dear; द्रष्टा – seer; सर्वप्रियतमः – dearest of all; सः अहम् – He am I; इति – thus; अवधारय – ascertain

24. *Know yourself to be the One for whose sake beings and things such as children and wealth are dear, who is the sole Seer and dearest of all. 'He am I' (So'ham) – ascertain thus and realise.*

In our present state of Consciousness, an average, ordinary man should feel that there are things that are dear to him. But if we carefully observe ourselves, we shall find that a thing is full of joy to one only when it is conducive to the individual's present mood. An object of joy can become a nuisance or a positive pain when the individual's physical environment, or his inner mood changes. The same object of joy, under different conditions, can itself give pain and aversion.

When tickled by a desire, our mind gets extremely agitated and on fulfilling that desire the mind becomes quiet and we experience a flash of joy. In fact, whenever the mind is quiet, joy or bliss is the experience. As it were, when the mind is hushed, the joy light, which is the very nature of the Self, gets a chance to beam out and the average man misunderstands that his happiness is due to the possession of the object.

It cannot be. If the object can provide happiness by itself under all conditions, whenever we gain that object it should give the same amount of happiness – just as fire burns, irrespective of the physical conditions or the mental mood of one who is touching the fire. Heat is its very nature. We similarly should never find joy as the nature of the object. An object which can give us joy at one time, can provide agony, sorrow or aversion under different conditions.

Again, if we still continue studying our behaviour we shall find that man is ever ready to throw away the sense objects when they are dangerous to his body, for man loves his body more than the sense objects outside him in the world around him.

When a painful ulcer is providing our mind insufferable sense of agony continuously, we run to a doctor and readily suggest to him to amputate the limb away, if need be. We are ready to sacrifice our body when it gives painful agitation to the mind, for we love our mind more than our body.

Our mental emotions and personal sentiments are readily discarded when they clash with our intellectual ideal, vision, decision or conviction. We are willing to give up our mind and its love and attachment when they clash with our intellect, for we seem to love our intellect more than our mind.

Thus viewed, the Seer (of the intellect-mind-body and the outer objects) seems to be the innermost Essence in us and we unknowingly entertain the greatest love for it. This Self (Ātman) is experienced as the very object of our supreme love (sarvapriyatama). This final seat of one's own Self, the Seer, is the ultimate Reality; 'He am I' (So'ham), thus assert again and again and come to realise It.

परप्रेमास्पदतया मा न भूवमहं सदा ।
भूयासमिति यो द्रष्टा सोऽहमित्यवधारय ॥२५॥

parapremāspadatayā mā na bhūvamahaṁ sadā,
bhūyāsamiti yo draṣṭā so'hamityavadhāraya. (25)

परमप्रेमास्पदतया – due to being liked; **मा** – no; **न** – not; **भुवम्** – am; **अहम्** – I; **सदा** – ever; **भूयासम्** – let be; **इति** – thus; **यः** – who; **द्रष्टा** – seer; **सः अहम्** – He am I; **इति** – thus; **अवधारय** – ascertain

25. Know yourself to be the One regarding whom there is always the anxiety, 'May I ever be; never cease to be' as this Seer is the dearest of all. 'He am I' thus assert and realise.

The essential Self in us is so dear to us that no one can ever conceive the idea, 'I cease to exist' or 'I shall cease to be.' In all the three periods of time 'I am' is the constant experience: hence, what the biologists declare as the self-preservation instinct – and so no one wants to end himself, or come to any harm, or ever cease to be. We are ready to sacrifice everything else, so that we may exist and continue to survive. In our ignorance at this moment, we consider ourselves to be the body-mind-intellect equipment. Hence I, the body demands my happiness through the objects. I, the mind, seeks its satisfaction through its emotion and I, the intellect, with its ideas and ideals. The misconceived ego in us is today the final seat of all our love, since we live identified with the ego-sense (jīvātmā) in us in our present state of spiritual ignorance.

Even in ourselves we have found how we are ready to throw up and readily sacrifice all the outer for the sake of the inner, and therefore the subtler layer of our personality. For the sake of our ideals, faith or desire, which are of the intellectual sheath, we find it so easy to sacrifice objects of the body and emotions of the mind. Thus, as we move into the deep depths in our personality, our love for the deeper and subtler increases over the outer and grosser. Naturally, we can conclude that the seat of our supreme love is the ultimate Self. It is for the sake of the Self that other things are loved by us.[1]

---

[1] *Bṛhadāraṇyaka-upaniṣad* – 1.4.8; and 2.4.5

This seer in us that sees and knows all the activities of the sense organs, mind and intellect, this 'Witnessing Consciousness' which is the supreme seat of all our love, is the Self.

'This Self am I' – (So'ham), thus assert again and again and come to awake to Its plenitude and realise It.

यः साक्षिलक्षणो बोधस्त्वंपदार्थः स उच्यते।
साक्षित्वमपि बोद्धृत्वमविकारितयात्मनः ॥२६॥

yaḥ sākṣilakṣaṇo bodhastvaṁpadārthaḥ sa ucyate,
sākṣitvamapi boddhṛtvamavikāritayātmanaḥ. (26)

यः साक्षिलक्षणः – who appears as Witness; बोधः – Consciousness; त्वम्पदार्थः – meant by the word 'Thou'; सः – he; उच्यते – said; साक्षित्वम् – witnesshood; अपि – also; बोद्धृत्वम् – illumining power; अविकारितया – being free from all modifications; आत्मनः – of the Self

26. The Consciousness, the 'Self' which appears as the Witness, is that which is meant by the word 'Thou'. Being free from all changes even the witnessing is nothing but the illumining power of the 'Self'.

It is the light of Consciousness, the 'Self' that illumines all experiences at the body-mind-intellect level and which ever remains in us as a Witness, uninvolved, yet, the Seer of all. This 'witness' existing as the experience in each embodied form is the essential factor indicated by term 'Thou' in the great commandment (Mahavākya) of the *Ṛg-Veda* 'That Thou Art.' (Tat Tvam Asi)[1]

Ordinary man fails to understand that the Self in its essential nature is nothing but 'Knowledge without objects' (jñānasvarūpa).

It is only as a result of our spiritual study, when we deeply reflect upon the great statements (Mahāvākya) that we get a glimpse of this significance. The term 'Thou' in the statement 'That Thou Art', in a relative sense is understood as the individual Self, the jīva. But in its deepest import the term 'Thou' points to the essential Self, pure Knowledge (jñānasvarūpa). The Consciousness, the Self, being the illuminator in all, at all times, this 'witnessing Consciousness' is called the Ātman.

The ocean itself is the essential nature (svarūpa) of all waves, ripples and bubbles recognised by us on its surface. Thus the ocean is the svarūpa of the waves. The Consciousness that plays in all experiences is the one light illuminating everything. Here, do not understand that the Self is the one who makes us

---

[1] *Chāndogya-upaniṣad* – 6.8.7

conscious of things; Self is the very essential nature (svarūpa) of the thoughts and objects, mind and sense organs.

In our day-to-day life we can never remain without perceptions and thoughts and they are lit up in our awareness by the light of the Self, the pure Knowledge in us. Thus, the Self appears to function as a witness in us. When the thoughts cease and all perceptions end, we can no longer consider the Self as a witness - for what is there for It to witness?

To lift the student from his present experience of 'conscious-thoughts, into the state of pure, thoughtless-Consciousness' the witness concept is made use of by the teachers in Vedānta. They call this concept, by a familiar term Witness, defining it as 'Self, illumining the thoughts and experiences.' The experiences are illusory when they cease since there are no more thoughts to illumine, it has to express itself as thoughtless-Consciousness, the essential state (svarūpa) of pure Knowledge (jñana). This state alone is the true nature, as the Self is ever devoid of all changes (Avikāritayā-Ātmanaḥ).

देहेन्द्रियमनः प्राणाहङ्कृतिभ्यो विलक्षणः।
प्रोज्झिताशेषषड्भावविकारस्त्वंपदाभिधः ॥२७॥

dehendriyamanaḥ prāṇāhaṅkṛtibhyo vilakṣaṇaḥ,
projjhitāśeṣaṣaḍbhāvavikārastvampadābhidhaḥ. (27)

देहेन्द्रियमनः प्राणाहङ्कृतिभ्यः – from the body, senses, mind, vital air and ego; विलक्षणः – distinct; प्रोज्झिताशेषषड्भावविकारः – absolutely free from the six modifications; त्वम्पदाभिधः – meaning of the term 'Thou'

27. Totally distinct from body, senses, mind, prāṇa, and ego is that which is the Self. Therefore, it is absolutely free from the six modifications, which all material things must necessarily undergo. This Self is the indicative meaning of the term 'Thou'.

Earlier, it was established that the term Thou is the witnessing Consciousness (sākṣi), which in its essential nature (svarūpa) is 'objectless-Knowledge' (jñāna). That this Self is distinct from the gross body and the subtle body and their respective objects, is briefly but thoroughly discussed here. The body and its sense organs, the mind and its creative forces and the ego, all of them exist and function only because of the touch of Consciousness, the Self; by themselves they are all inert and insentient matter. It only appears that the gross body and the subtle body are conscious and alive, that they can intelligently think and efficiently function all by themselves. But as they are made of matter they should be, by their very nature, ever inert. Yet, due to our ignorance, we accept that they do function by themselves. Only on closer study can we come to realise that their consciousness and dynamism are the play of the 'light of the Self.'

While playing upon the ever-changing flux of matter, this light of the Self seems to be also ever-changing. The Self is changeless (avikāri). The modifications are the destiny of matter alone. Every material form in the universe must necessarily go through six unavoidable stages of modification (shaḍ-bhāva) during its existence – birth, existence, growth, decay, disease and death. The changeless Self has none of these modifications (avikāraḥ) in it. The very mind, intellect, thoughts and ego, constituting the subtle body, even within a given gross body, keeps on changing under the compulsion of the law of modification unavoidable in the world of matter.

The Consciousness is ever one and changeless, illumining in every bosom all changes experienced by the individual, under all conditions, at all places and times, both in bondage and Liberation as the Self (nirvikāra). Hence, the spiritual centre, the Self, has to be ever indicated as distinct from all things known to us now (vilakṣaṇa). This Self, entirely distinct from the gross and subtle bodies and all their modifications, this light of Consciousness is the deeper significance of the term 'Thou' in the Mahāvākya. It, identified with the delusory equipment comes to sport as the jīva. On Self-realisation, It rediscovers itself to be as the pure Self. Subjectively assert yourself that you are this pure Self and realise your magnificent glory, the true Being.

With this verse the section that discriminates the Self, by showing it as distinctively different from the gross and the subtle body, is concluded. This examination, for the purpose of study, was started with verse 17. Here Śaṅkara concludes his discourse upon the meaning of the term 'Thou' (Tvam) in the commandment, and from the following verse the Guru starts his discussion upon the, term 'That' (Tat).

'Thou' is the infinite Self functioning as the Witness of the inner-equipment and their functions. While 'That' is the infinite Self functioning as a Witness of māyā and all her modifications. Verses 28 - 36 explain for our contemplation the deeper significance of 'That'.

त्वमर्थमेवं निश्चित्य तदर्थं चिन्तयेत्पुनः ।
अतद्व्यावृत्तिरूपेण साक्षाद्विधिमुखेन च ॥२८ ॥

tvamarthamevaṁ niścitya tadarthaṁ cintayetpunaḥ,
atadvyāvṛttirūpeṇa sākṣādvidhimukhena ca. (28)

त्वमर्थम् – the meaning of the term 'Thou'; एवम् – thus; निश्चित्य – having ascertained; तदर्थम् – meaning of the term 'That'; चिन्तयेत् – should reflect; पुनः – again; अतद्व्यावृत्तिरूपेण – by the method of negation; साक्षात् विधिमुखेन च – and by the direct method of scriptural assertion

28. Having thus ascertained the meaning of the term 'Thou' one should reflect upon what is meant by the word 'That' employing both the method of negation and also the direct method of scriptural assertion.

The obvious but superficial understanding of the term 'Thou' is the egocentric individual in us, the jīva. This is the word meaning, but the deeper suggestion is that it is the Self, and this was exhaustively expounded so far. This realisation brings the student fully prepared for the journey on the path to his own personal and direct experience.

Remaining in the non-apprehension of Reality, for many many aeons, the jīva now fails to readily comprehend the suggestive meaning of the term 'Thou' in the Mahāvākya. Continuous and repeated reflections, logical discussions and subtle independent ponderings are all necessary to recognise the depth-meaning of the term 'Thou'.

In order to establish firmly the essential indicative meaning of the term 'Thou' it will be helpful if we strive to apprehend the full import of the term 'That' (Tat) in the declaration 'That Thou Art.' This term is expounded and brought to the student's direct and immediate comprehension by the Upaniṣads, consistently employing two different techniques – the method of negation (niṣedha) of what are not really the infinite substratum of the universe, 'That' and also the method of assertion (vidhi), wherein directly the scriptures have ascertained the infinite nature of 'That' the Brahman. A sincere student must repeatedly contemplate upon the essence behind the universe taking advantage of both these techniques.

In the relative world of finite experience, the term 'Thou' indicates the limited creature, the arrogant ego, that entertains the vanity that he is the 'doer' (kartā) and the 'experiencer,' (bhoktā), At this juncture, from the standpoint of the jīva, 'That' can mean only the Lord (Īśvara), who had created the world and is providing the ego with all its experiences, as ordered by the quality of his own past actions. But in the absolute sense, the Consciousness that is the Self (Ātman) in you is the 'Self' everywhere, the supreme Self, (Brahman).

The individual 'Self', the jīva, and the universal Self, Īśvara, are both the expressions of the one infinite Self (Brahman). The ego (jīva) and the Lord (Īśvara) are apparently different, apparently separate and indescribably distinct from each other only because of the differences in their equipment. The Self, the Supreme, expressed in avidyā is jīva, while when the same supreme Self expresses in māyā becomes Īśvara. When the avidyā in us is eliminated, when the jīva rises above its non-apprehension and consequent misapprehensions, the māyā also is crossed. The essence behind the jīva and Īśvara is apprehended then, in one blindening flash of realisation, as the one infinite mass of pure Consciousness.

The various declarations of the Upaniṣads, that indicate the depth-meaning of this term, prescribe for us the lines of enquiries and investigations to be undertaken, in order to successfully reflect upon and ascertain the subtle suggestions enshrined in the pregnant suggestions of the term 'That.'[1]

The following are two verses each giving an example of the negation style and the assertion style employed effectively in indicating the meaning of the term 'That' the Brahman.

[1] 'Neither gross nor subtle...' - *Bṛhadāraṇyaka-upaniṣad* – 3.8.8 *Taittirīya-upaniṣad* – 2.1.1) and 3.6.1)

निरस्ताशेषसंसारदोषोऽस्थूलादिलक्षणः ।
अदृश्यत्वादिगुणकः पराकृततमोमलः ॥२९॥

nirastāśeṣasaṁsāradoṣo'sthūlādilakṣaṇaḥ,
adṛśyatvādiguṇakaḥ parākṛtatamomalaḥ. (29)

निरस्ताशेषसंसारदोषः – free from all the impurities of saṁsāra; **अस्थूलादिलक्षणः** – defined by the terms such as 'not gross' and so on; **अदृश्यत्वादिगुणकः** – having the qualities of imperceptibility and so on; **पराकृततमोमलः** – beyond all darkness created by ignorance

29. 'That' which is free from all the impurities of the saṁsāra; 'That' which is defined by the Upaniṣads as, 'not gross and so on, having the qualities of imperceptible and so on, that is beyond all darkness created by ignorance.'

The direct meaning (vācyārtha) of 'Thou' (Tvam) is jīva, but its indicative meaning (lakṣyārtha) is the Consciousness functioning as the 'Witness' in all experiences of every living being. Similarly, the direct meaning (vācyārtha) of the term 'That' (Tat) is Īśvara, who is also in saṁsāra as He has the māyā for His equipment. The supreme Self functioning through 'māyā'[1] is Īśvara and through 'ignorance' is jīva.[2]

No doubt, relatively speaking, Īśvara as the omnipotent and omniscient is more free, respondent, and glorious, as compared with the limited and miserable ego, that is jīva, yet even Īśvara is but a limited expression of the Self, as He functions through māyā. The indicative meaning (laksyārtha) of Īśvara (Tat) is the essence in Him – which is entirely free from māyā – the pure infinite Self. Thus, 'That' is described here as a factor 'which is absolutely free from all impurities of saṁsāra the transmigratory existence.'[3] In short, Brahman is the laksyārtha of 'Īśvara'. Every creature (jīva) has its gross, subtle and the causal bodies. Īśvara has also these three bodies – the macrocosmic gross body will be Īśvara's body (Virāṭa); the total subtle body is the Hiraṇyagarbha and total causal body, representing the total unmanifested vāsanās is Īśvara. But beyond all bodies is the Essence, the Brahman which cannot be conditioned by these equipments and their limitations.

---

[1] Macrocosmic avidyā is māyā.

[2] Microcosmic non-apprehension of the Self is avidyā (ignorance).

[3] *Iśāvāsya-upaniṣad* – 8

The terms of negation used in the Upaniṣads, indicate that these relative measurements (gross, subtle, big, short, long and so on) in the Absolute have no meaning. Truth lies beyond the intellect. Brahman is, therefore, indicated as beyond all our familiar intellectual estimation and descriptions.[1]

Forms and colours are seen, they belong to the gross body. Behind the endless perceivable qualities of the gross, revels the pure Self, the illuminator of all, the one seer in all perceptions. Through our sense organs we perceive the gross world of qualities, and this perception of plurality ceases to be in the 'experience' of the one infinite Self. When the student realises this, the aim and purpose of Vedānta is achieved. The Self is not available as an object for any of our senses or mind, to perceive.

Again, in this Self there can be no touch of the impurities of ignorance, agitations of the mind (vikṣepa) and veiling of the intellect (āvaraṇa).

[1] The *Bṛhadāraṇyaka-upaniṣad* describes the Self as 'neither gross nor subtle, neither short nor long' (3.8.8). Similarly, *Muṇḍakopaniṣad* (1.1.6) describes the Self as imperceptible, (adreśya-agrāhya-agotra-avarṇam). In this language of negation, the great seat of Reality and its nature are indicated by the scriptures.

Beyond all darkness is the ever-effulgent Self, the Consciousness.[1]

Thus, Brahman, which is the depth-meaning of the term 'That' (Tat) is shown here by the language of negations (niṣedha) used by the Upaniṣads.

In the following verse, the same Brahman is discussed by the ṛṣis of the Upaniṣads in the language of assertion (vidhi).

[1] ādityavarṇaṁ tamasaḥ parastāt – *Bhagavad-gītā*-8.9

निरस्तातिशयानन्दः सत्यप्रज्ञानविग्रहः ।
सत्तास्वलक्षणः पूर्णः परमात्मेति गीयते ॥३० ॥

nirastātiśayānandaḥ satyaprajñānavigrahaḥ,
sattāsvalakṣaṇaḥ pūrṇaḥ paramātmeti gīyate. (30)

निरस्तातिशयानन्दः – having no greater Bliss than Itself ; सत्यप्रज्ञानविग्रहः – embodiment of eternal Consciousness; सत्तास्वलक्षणः – having 'Existence' for its specific definition; पूर्णः – all-pervading; परमात्मेति गीयते – declared by the term 'supreme Being' ('That')

30. Having no greater Bliss than Itself, a pure embodiment of eternal Consciousness and having Existence for its specific definition, is the all-pervading Being. This is the meaning indicated by the term That, so the scriptures declare in their songs.

In the *Taittirīya-upaniṣad,* the ṛṣi gives a list of relatively higher and higher happiness and concludes that the happiness of the Man of Perfection, living the experience of Brahman, is more than 'even a hundred Creators[1].' The Brahman, the all-pervading universal Self, indicated by the term 'That' is thus declared by the scriptures as 'having no greater Bliss than Itself.' The supreme Self is 'an embodiment of eternal Consciousness[2].' The Brahman, the universal Self indicated by the term 'That' is thus declared by the scriptures as having 'no greater Bliss than Itself.'

This supreme Self is an undifferentiated mass of eternal Consciousness is pointed out in the Upaniṣad as 'Truth, Knowledge, Infinite.'[3] It is the pure Consciousness, that ever remains the same, unchanged in all the three periods of time, hence satya.

This supreme Self is an embodiment of eternal Consciousness. Consciousness, as the very light in our intellect, illumines all our thoughts and it is called Prajñānam.[4] The ṛṣi in *Aitareya-upaniṣad* defines the 'Self' as Prajñānam Brahma.

[1] *Taittirīya-upaniṣad* 2.8.4

[2] 'satyam jñānam anantam brahma'- *Taittirīya-upaniṣad* 2.1.1

[3] 'satyam-jñānam-anantam brahma' - *Taittirīya-upaniṣad* 2.1.1

[4] *Aitareya-upaniṣad* 3.1.3

The Self is Existence. The world of names and forms exists in our experience. This pure Existence (not the items that constitute experiences) is the play of the Self, while the names and forms, their properties and functions are all illusions built up and sustained by the mind, tickled by the vāsanās (avidyā). This principle of Existence that sports in everything, always, everywhere, within and without, this Existence (sattā) is only positive and most direct definition (svalakṣaṇa). Therefore Existence becomes the most direct and specific definition of the Self.

The eternal Self is ever-full (Pūrṇa); it is Unlimited and Infinite.[1] In all names and forms Existence expresses as 'existence of' the thing and as things change 'existence of' the things also apparently changes. The light playing upon an object, should take the shape of the object, and if the shape changes, the light also must change. That is why the poets often sing, sunlight dancing upon the ocean. In fact, the waves alone dance but sunlight while playing upon them appears to be dancing.

[1] *Bṛhadāraṇyaka-upaniṣad* – 5.1.1

The universal Self, Brahman, is the one Existence that is unconditioned by the nature and quality of the objects in the illusory universe of names and forms.

The tree beyond your window exists. When the tree is cut down, the fallen trunk exists. When it is sawed into planks, the trunk does not, but the planks exist. The planks are made into furniture pieces, planks do not, but the furniture pieces exist. Thus 'Existence' in the tree did not ever change in the different changes that we just mentioned. This pure Existence is ever-full (pūrṇa). Everything finite has distinctions within itself (svagata bheda)[1] distinction between different species (vijātīya bheda)[2] and there are distinctions from one species to another in the same species (sajātīya bheda)[3]. That which has no such distinctions and so remains the same, in all three periods of time, is considered as ever-full (pari-pūrṇa).

For example:

[1] The head is not like the hands, the hands are not like the legs.

[2] The horse is not like the cow and the cow is different from the birds.

[3] The brown, the black, the red cow.

Here in this verse we have an honest attempt of ṛṣis in defining the supreme Truth through the method of direct assertion. It is Existence; It is all-full.

Even here, please note that the assertive statements are themselves used only as indications to what this Truth is in us. They are not descriptions of the Reality. Indeed, finite words cannot express the Infinite.

सर्वज्ञत्वं परेशत्वं तथा सम्पूर्णशक्तिता ।
वेदैः समर्थ्यते यस्य तद्ब्रह्मेत्यवधारय ॥३१ ॥

sarvajñatvaṁ pareśatvaṁ tathā sampūrṇaśaktitā,
vedaiḥ samarthyate yasya tadbrahmetyavadhāraya. (31)

सर्वज्ञत्वम् – being all-knowing; परेशत्वम् – being supreme Lord; तथा – so also; सम्पूर्णशक्तिता – being all-powerful; वेदैः – by the scriptures; समर्थ्यते – proved; यस्य – whose; तद्ब्रह्म – That is Brahman; इति – thus; अवधारय – ascertain

31. That which is proved in the Vedas as all-knowing, all-powerful and supreme Lord, is Itself the infinite Brahman, make sure of that Brahman in your own understanding.

In these following six verses, Śaṅkara expounds through various pointers, the supreme Brahman, the one infinite substratum for the entire illusions of plurality. In producing or creating anything, three different kinds of causes come into play – the material cause, the instrumental cause and the efficient cause.

In the case of making a mud pot, the mud is the material cause, the wheel of the potter is the instrumental cause and the pot maker is the efficient cause. It is evidently clear that when the created pot gets broken the pot maker or the mud suffers no destruction. The mud may get washed off but the pot maker is not affected at all. Similarly, when the world of plurality is destroyed, or when changes take place in the world of things and beings, the efficient cause behind them is not affected in the least.

Here then, is yet another difference to be noticed. In our example, the pot maker is different from mud and the wheel, but in the case of the pluralistic world, Brahman is, at one and the same time, the material, instrumental and efficient cause, as in the case of a dream, the waking mind is at once the material, instrumental and the intelligent cause.

In this verse under review, Brahman is declared as the efficient cause (nimitta kāraṇa), and in the following five verses the supreme Brahman is shown as the very material cause (upādāna) for the creation of the delusory world.

In the earlier verses, through the method of negation[1] and through the method of assertion[2] the pure Brahman, potential with the universe of multiplicity, was described. In this section of six verses[3], the relative Self (kārya-Brahman) in its universal expressions is expounded. It is Brahman as Īśvara, the Lord of the universe (Jagadīsvara). Brahman seen through 'māyā' is the Lord (Īśvara) and when expressing through ignorance (avidyā) becomes the creature (jīva). Thus, to point out the highest Truth, in and through its expressions in the equipments of the macrocosm (samaṣṭi) and microcosm (vyaṣṭi), is a way of bringing the student's entire attention to the Self within himself. Thus that which the scriptures have declared as Īśvara is Brahman and the Brahman is again that which is expressed as the universe of names and forms.

Brahman, expressing through māyā[4] is Īśvara and Īśvara is master of māyā, with which He manifests as all-knowing and all-powerful. But

[1] Verse 29

[2] Verse 30

[3] Verse 31-36

[4] Macrocosmic universal vāsanās, the total causal-body - māyā.

when the supreme Self expresses through avidyā,[1] He is the individualised Self, the jīva, and as jīva he is a slave to avidyā and He manifests as ignorant and powerless, weak and sorrow-ridden, confused and dejected.

Yet, devoid of the equipments of Māyā and avidyā, both Īśvara and jīva are nothing but the supreme Self, which is the indicative meaning (lakṣyārtha) of all the terms: creature-world-creator (jīva-jagat-Īśvara).

Brahman and Īśvara are not two factors, but when the supreme Consciousness is at rest it is Brahman, and in dynamic expression Brahman itself sports as Īśvara. In moments of total meditation, the individual mind halts and its illusory flutterings, thoughts cease. Avidyā ends and the pure māyāless Brahman is comprehended and realised as the jīva's own real nature.

In avidyā, jīva is ever under the stress of its endless mental agitations (vikṣepa) and intellectual veiling (āvaraṇa), and so, limited in its knowledge

---

[1] Microcosmic individual vāsanās, a single causal-body. avidyā

and power (sarvajñatvam and para-īśatvam). In māyā, Īśvara is not agitated nor veiled and therefore, His glories manifest in Him and we recognise Him as all-knowing and all-powerful.

To contemplate upon these ideas and to ascertain and finally to make sure of this essential oneness of you, your world and Īśvara in Brahman, is the supreme fulfilment of life, the subtle goal of Vedānta, the loving anxiety of all scriptures of the world.

यज्ज्ञानात्सर्वविज्ञानं श्रुतिषु प्रतिपादितम् ।
मृदाद्यनेकदृष्टान्तैस्तद्ब्रह्मेत्यवधारय ॥३२ ॥

yajjñānātsarvavijñānaṁ śrutiṣu pratipāditam,
mṛdādyanekadṛṣṭāntaistadbrahmetyavadhāraya. (32)

यज्ज्ञानात्सर्वविज्ञानम् – knowing which all else becomes known; श्रुतिषु – in the scriptures; प्रतिपादितम् – discussed; मृदाद्यनेकदृष्टान्तैः – through examples of mud and so on; तद्ब्रह्म – That is Brahman; इति – thus; अवधारय – ascertain

32. That which the scriptures have discussed through examples of mud and so on, as that by knowing which all else will become known, make sure of that Brahman in your understanding.

Here Śaṅkara takes the scriptural[1] examples to prove that the effects are the cause itself in different forms. The pot, jug, plate, cup and so on are all mud itself in different forms; their forms, names, functions, and uses are different and they are impermanent also. But mud, the cause, is permanent and ever the

[1] *Chāndogya-upaniṣad* – 6.1.4 to 6

same. Mud, the cause, existed even before the pot was made. The mud remained all the time as the 'heart' of the pot.

When the pot breaks, the mud survives. Similarly, this universe which is ever-changing, has also a changeless cause upon which all changes are playing; that is Brahman.

By knowing the essential nature of the cause, the essential nature of the effects are known; in mud there are no cups, pots and so on. By knowing the mud, all effects rising from mud are known. Similarly, in Brahman, there is nothing else other than Itself to know and since everything apparently rises from It, everything becomes known when the pure Knowledge, the Absolute, is realised. Thus, by knowing the efficient cause (nimitta kāraṇa), which is other than the effects, we cannot fully understand the product. But the material cause (upādāna kāraṇa) is ever with the effect and so knowing it, we can know the 'heart' of all things made of it.

By knowing the goldsmith, we do not understand the ornaments; if we know gold, the 'heart' of all ornaments is immediately known. Brahman is the upādāna kāraṇa (material cause) for the universe. By knowing the eternal Self we can know the essence in each one of us. We hereby realise the permanent Reality behind the ever-changing universe of names and forms.

Make sure of this Brahman in your direct understanding.

यदानन्त्यं प्रतिज्ञाय श्रुतिस्तत्सिद्धये जगौ ।
तत्कार्यत्वं प्रपञ्चस्य तद्ब्रह्मेत्यवधारय ॥३३॥

yadānantyaṁ pratijñāya śrutistatsiddhaye jagau,
tatkāryatvaṁ prapañcasya tadbrahmetyavadhāraya. (33)

यदानन्त्यम् – which is limitless; प्रतिज्ञाय – propose; श्रुतिः – scripture; तत्सिद्धये – to prove; जगौ – in order to support; तत्कार्यत्वम् – as its effects; प्रपञ्चस्य – of the world; तद्ब्रह्म – That is Brahman; इति – thus; अवधारय – ascertain

33. That which the scriptures propose to prove as limitless and in order to support that proposition, called the world of plurality as Its effects, make sure of that Brahman in your understanding.

Cause is always more subtle and so more pervasive than the effects. He who has cultivated in himself all the required predispositions is therefore, a fully qualified student. To him the idea that the Brahman is the substratum for the world of multiplicity is, indeed, easy to grasp, through various examples such as the rope and the serpent, the ghost in the post, the silveriness in the mother-of-pearls. The anxiety of the scriptures (śāstra) is to help the gross type of seekers to understand the Reality.

A seeker who is not fully prepared within to grasp at once the nature of Brahman and realise It is relatively dense, meaning he has in him more vāsanās and consequently, more restlessness in his mind. By the mind, of course, one recognises the world of plurality and an intelligent man knows that the cosmos spread around him is indeed vast and infinite, in all its endless dimensions. To make him comprehend that the Brahman is Infinite, the ṛṣis were compelled to explain to him that the universe is an 'effect' from the Brahman; as an effect is nothing other than its own cause. The world is but Brahman in manifestation.

When this idea is fully appreciated by the relatively dull seeker, it would be easier for him to recognise, soon enough, that the supreme Brahman is the very substratum for the entire illusory world of names and forms. This is the intelligent intention in, the anxious purpose for and the loving urgency of all the descriptions of creation in the Upaniṣads.

That which is the One without a second (advaita), in its own pure essential nature, is ever Itself. When It is viewed through the perceived world or apparent multiplicity, it sports in our understanding as the Infinite (ananta) cause of the universe.

There is no contradiction in defining Brahman by these two indicative terms: 'non-dual' (advaita) and the 'Infinite' (ananta). That from which the world of names and forms arise, in which they apparently exist and play, and without which the world can never exist, 'That' understand to be Brahman.

Through our mental agitations, caused by the turbulence of our likes and dislikes, we now live firmly convinced of the reality of the pluralistic world. This is the source of all our sorrows and the agony of the world of beings.

May we end this 'misapprehension' in us, and come to realise the world of things and beings as merely an apparent illusory expression of Brahman. And this infinite Consciousness alone is, the only Reality, the Truth. It revels as the Self in us, the spring of Consciousness in our bosom; 'That' from which all our thoughts wave up, play, dance and disappear. Make sure of that Brahman in your understanding.

विजिज्ञास्यतया यच्च वेदान्तेषु मुमुक्षुभिः ।
समर्थ्यतेऽतियत्नेन तद्ब्रह्मेत्यवधारय ॥३४ ॥

vijijñāsyatayā yacca vedānteṣu mumukṣubhiḥ,
samarthyate'tiyatnena tadbrahmetyavadhāraya. (34)

विजिज्ञास्यतया – as object of contemplation; **यत्** – that; **च** – and; **वेदान्तेषु** – in the Upaniṣads; **मुमुक्षिभिः** – by seekers of Liberation; **समर्थ्यते** – establish; **अतियत्नेन** – with effort; **तद्ब्रह्म** – That is Brahman; **इति** – thus; **अवधारय** – ascertain

34. That which the Upaniṣads clearly establish as the sole object of deep contemplation for those who are sincere seekers of Liberation, make sure of that Brahman in your understanding.

We have a clear indication in the *Taittirīya-upaniṣad* of what must be the theme of contemplation for one who is anxious for the Liberation of his personality, from the thraldom of his own matter vestures - body, mind and intellect.

The Upaniṣad insists clearly that we must contemplate upon 'that' from which all the perceived world of things and beings have risen, 'That' in which they continue to exist and in the end, 'That' into which all merge back (in dissolution).[1] That is the point of attention for all deep and continuous contemplation.

The mud is the material cause (upādāna kāraṇa) for all pots – all pots are born from mud, exist in mud and when broken, go back to be the mud. Similarly, Brahman is shown here as the upādāna kāraṇa of the universe, for the purpose of contemplation by the limited human mind.

By thus contemplating upon that which is ever present everywhere, which is the essence in every form, the seeker's entire attention gets lifted from the world of plurality and it gets settled upon the Self within. The mental agitations then cease. thoughts end. The mind halts. The ego disappears into the vision of the Supreme – in a most direct and subjective Experience Divine.

Make sure of that Brahman in your understanding.

---

[1] *yato vā imani bhūtani jāyante, yena jātāni jīvanti, yat-prayantya-bhisamviśanti; tadvijijñāsasva. – Taittirīya-upaniṣad* – 3.1.1

जीवात्मना प्रवेशश्च नियन्तृत्वं च तान् प्रति ।
श्रूयते यस्य वेदेषु तद्ब्रह्मेत्यवधारय ॥३५ ॥

jīvātmanā praveśaśca niyantṛtvaṁ ca tān prati,
śrūyate yasya vedeṣu tadbrahmetyavadhāraya. (35)

जीवात्मना प्रवेशः – entering as the individual Self; च – and; नियन्तृत्वम् – being the controller; च – and; तान् प्रति – towards them; श्रूयते यस्य – that which is heard of; वेदेषु – in the Vedas; तद्ब्रह्म – That is Brahman; इति – thus; अवधारय – ascertain

35. That which is heard of in the Vedas 'as having entered each creature as its individualised Self', and which is known, from the same sources, to be their controller, make sure of that Brahman in your understanding.

In the Upaniṣads, while describing the creation process, the ṛṣi declares that, having created the best among the creatures – man – the infinite Self 'entered' him to enjoy through the perfect equipments so created. 'He contemplated and created all these, then He himself entered.'[1]

Brahman, the infinite creative potential, identifying with Its own potential, 'became' God; thereafter, God, in his impatience to create, became the Creator; the Creator created the world of things and beings, a fulfilment of His creative urge. But having created, He identified, 'entered' into the created form and became a creature, you, the individualised ego.

This 'entry' is only in the form of Its own 'reflection' (ābhāsa) in the individual mind-intellect equipment, and this Consciousness, playing upon thoughts (cidābhāsa), becomes the individual ego. As an ego, he suffers the sorrows and imperfections of saṁsāra; the reflection of the sun will have to dance when the surface of the waters gets disturbed by the breeze around it.

When this delusory identification in an individual ends, he realises the pure, unconditioned Reality to be his own true nature – true Being.

---

[1] *'idaṁ saravamasṛjata, yadidaṁ kiṁca,*
tatsṛṣṭvā, tadevānuprāviśat.' – *Taittrīya-upa*niṣad – 2.6.1

Not only does Brahman thus sport, as though It has entered the created equipment and has become a creature, but It, as the Self, indeed rules the inner world of elements and their might. The *Bṛhadāraṇyaka-upaniṣad,* in its *Antaryāmi Brāhmaṇa,* says 'remaining within the earth and the five elements, it drives their individual presiding deities (devatās) – 'powers' – according to some definite and precise scientific laws.'[1]

That which having created the creatures and 'entered' to become the individual Self, that which remaining in the elemental forces, by Its mere presence controls, regulates and governs all their behaviour into a very precise scientific pattern, is the eternal Self. Make sure of that Brahman in your understanding.

---

[1] *yaḥ pṛthivyāṁ tiṣṭhan.... pṛthivīmantarobhrayati*

कर्मणां फलदातृत्वम् यस्यैव श्रूयते श्रुतौ ।
जीवानां हेतुकर्तृत्वं तद्ब्रह्मेत्यवधारय ॥३६ ॥

karmaṇāṁ phaladātṛtvam yasyaiva śrūyate śrutau,
jīvānāṁ hetukartṛtvaṁ tadbrahmetyavadhāraya. (36)

कर्मणाम् – of actions; फलदातृत्वम् – paymaster; यस्य – whose; एव – alone; श्रूयते – declared; श्रुतौ – in the Upaniṣads; जीवानाम् – of the individual Self; हेतुकर्तृत्वम् – as the agent (prompter) in actions; तद्ब्रह्म – That is Brahman; इति – thus; अवधारय – ascertain

36. That which the Upaniṣads declare as the sole paymaster[1] for all actions and as the very agent (prompter[2]) in all actions, performed by[3] each individual ego, make sure of that Brahman in your understanding.

'No living creature can ever remain without activity, even for a single moment.'[4] Actions are

1 *Iśāvāsya-upaniṣad*-8

2 *Bṛhadāraṇyaka-upaniṣad* – 2.3.4 and *Kauṣitaki-upaniṣad*-3.8

3 *Bṛhadāraṇyaka-upaniṣad* –2.3.3

4 *'Na hi kaścit-kṣaṇamapi jātu tiṣṭhatya-karmakṛt.'* – *Gītā*-3.5

good or bad and accordingly, the individual ego has to experience their fruits of joy or sorrow. The results of actions depend not only upon the external actions, but the doer's inner mood and his intentions. These factors are intimately governed and guided by faith, sincerity, fortitude, understanding, the type of personality of the doer and a hundred other subtle and sensitive psychological factors. Thus, the end result of apparently same actions, undertaken by a host of people, are often found different from individual to individual. Like a highly competent computer, the result of each action is to be carefully calculated with all these hundreds of complementary data to finally determine the end result of each action (karma-phala). This is indeed confusing, even for the greatest of thinkers and scholars among the mortals.[1]

This mighty Intelligence that unerringly determines and justly distributes the exact results of action[2] is the Brahman playing through māyā, the Lord of the universe, Jagadīśvara. This Īśvara not only provides each with the exact results of

---

[1] *Kiṁ karma kiṁ-akarmeti kavayo'pyatra mohitāḥ.* – *Gītā*-4.16

[2] karmaphaladātā

his actions, but again, He is the one who comes to express in the mind and intellect of each bosom, as the ego and its vain glorious attitude that 'I am doer' in all actions.[1]

Make sure of that Brahman in your understanding. The discussion of the term 'That' (Tat) is concluded here.

The meaning of the statement 'That Thou Art' is expounded to indicate the invisible Existence Knowledge-Bliss (Self) from verse 37 through verse 41.

In order to determine the oneness of the Self in us (Ātman) and the Self everywhere (Brahman), the teacher continues his discourse with the following verse.

[1] Brahman functioning through avidyā is the ego, the jīvātmā – the ego in its ignorance has the false notions such as 'doer am I' (kartā) and 'enjoyer am I', (bhoktā).

तत्त्वंपदार्थौ निर्णीतौ वाक्यार्थश्चिन्त्यतेऽधुना ।
तादात्म्यमत्र वाक्यार्थस्तयोरेव पदार्थयोः ॥३७ ॥

tattvampadārthau nirṇītau vākyārthaścintyate'dhunā,
tādātmyamatra vākyārthastayoreva padārthayoḥ. **(37)**

तत्त्वम्पदार्थौ – the meaning of the terms 'That' and 'Thou'; निर्णीतौ – determined; वाक्यार्थः – the meaning of the statement ('That Thou Art'); चिन्त्यते – thought over; अधुना – now; तादात्म्यम् – identity; अत्र – here; वाक्यार्थः – meaning; तयोः – their; एव – alone; पदार्थयोः – the meaning of the terms

37. The meaning of the terms 'That' and 'Thou' have been discussed and finally determined. Now we shall discuss the meaning of the commandment (Mahāvākya) 'That Thou Art.' In this, the total identity of the meanings of 'That' and 'Thou' alone is shown.

Up to now, the word meanings of the terms 'Thou' and 'That' in the Mahāvākya, 'That Thou Art' were explained to show that they do not stand for the jīva and Īśvara (the vācyārtha), but these words connote (lakṣyārtha) the Self that illumines as a Witness of the thoughts and actions (Thou) and the pure Brahman (That) without the veilings of māyā.

When the direct word meaning (vācyārtha) is not sufficient to bring out fully the pregnant import of the scriptures, the suggestive meaning (lakṣyārtha) is taken by the intelligent student everywhere. The entire statement (Mahāvākya) 'That Thou Art' is indicative of the oneness (ekatā) of 'That' and 'Thou'– a total identity between the individual Self and the universal Self. By again and again contemplating upon the deep meaning of the Mahāvākya, all the doubts (saṁśaya) and all false conclusions (viparīta jñāna)[1] in the mind are removed.

The word meaning, no doubt, clarifies the idea which the individual word screams aloud, but in the context of a given sentence, often words may come to express much more than their usual dictionary word meanings. This total meaning of the sentence is

---

[1] Doubt (saṁśaya) and false conclusions (viparīta jñāna) are some of the deep-rooted mental blocks, because of which an individual gets totally walled away from gaining a clear and direct experience of the Self. These are some of the most terrible mental blocks which permanently hold the mind in leash from gaining an intimate spiritual vision and direct realisation of the Self.

called 'vākyārtha'. The direct word meaning here is: 'Thou' (Tvam) is the jīva, and 'That' (Tat) is Īśvara. But how can these two, the microcosm (vyaṣṭi) and the macrocosm (samaṣṭi) be ever one and the same? Yet, this sameness is indicated with 'the meaning of the total sentence' (vākyārtha), 'That Thou Art.' The scripture wants to eloquently indicate that these two different factors are the same in essence; this oneness and their essential identity, is subtly suggested by the import of the word, 'Art'.

This process of indicating the two terms 'Thou' and 'That' first as distinctly different, as the individual Self, (jīva) and as the Lord of creatures, Īśvara, then to assert their oneness, in their mutual identity, is to help the confused and the ignorant student to realise the supreme one infinite Self. The Brahman, seen as expressed through māyā, is Īśvara (That); the same Brahman, perceived as functioning through the inner equipments of an individual (avidyā) is the individual Self, the ego – the jīva (Thou).

How to logically arrive at the depth-meaning of this simple looking statements of Vedas is demonstrated in the following verse.

संसर्गो वा विशिष्टो वा वाक्यार्थो नात्र सम्मतः ।
अखण्डैकरसत्वेन वाक्यार्थो विदुषां मतः ॥३८ ॥

saṁsargo vā viśiṣṭo vā vākyārtho nātra sammataḥ,
akhaṇḍaikarasatvena vākyārtho viduṣāṁ mataḥ. (38)

संसर्गः – (as) sequence of meaning; वा – or; विशिष्टः – (as) qualified by something; वा – or; वाक्यार्थः – meaning of the sentence; न – not; अत्र – here; सम्मतः – accepted (arrived at); अखण्डैकरसत्वेन – as consisting of unbroken Bliss; वाक्यार्थः – meaning of the statement; विदुषां मतः – according to the wise

38. What is meant by the sentence – commandment – ('That Thou Art') is not arrived at, either through its 'sequence of meaning' or as 'qualified by something.' An indivisible Being, consisting of Bliss only, 'this alone is the meaning of the sentence, according to the wise.'

In understanding the meaning of the sentence, we may try to understand the sense from the 'sequence of meaning' (saṁsarga) expressed by the words 'I was there and I heard your discourse.' Here, the sequence of word meaning gives you the sense of the sentence; the listener of this sentence arrived at its sense merely on the strength of the 'sequence of words' (saṁsarga) and the sum total of their meanings. But in the sentence 'I was in that beautiful garden and I clearly heard all your eloquent discourses' the listener gathers the meaning, not only from the mere sequence (saṁsarga), but also from an intelligent appreciation of the qualifications (viśeṣaṇa) and the objects qualified (viśeṣya). Both these ordinary means of arriving at the total sense of a sentence, are not possible in reaching the depth meaning of the Mahāvākya, 'That Thou Art.'

The great men of spiritual experience and direct vision unanimously declare that there is a mutual identity between the individual Self (jīva) and the universal Self (Īśvara). This intimate identity (tādātmya) points out to the oneness of all names and forms with the supreme Self (Brahman). This meaning alone will be in line with the lived experience of the mystics, the ṛṣis. Thus, the witnessing Self within (Tvam) and the infinite Self, Brahman (Tat) are both identical and therefore the same, is the depth-meaning (lakṣyārtha) of the Mahāvākya, 'That Thou Art.' This is the accepted opinion (mataḥ), of the wise (viduṣāṁ).

This suggestive meaning, acknowledged by the wise men of full spiritual experience, is made vividly clear in the following verse.

प्रत्यग्बोधो य आभाति सोऽद्वयानन्दलक्षणः।
अद्वयानन्दरूपश्च प्रत्यग्बोधैकलक्षणः॥३९॥

pratyagbodho ya ābhāti so'dvayānandalakṣaṇaḥ,
advayānandarūpaśca pratyagbodhaikalakṣaṇaḥ. (39)

प्रत्यग्बोधः – Consciousness within; यः – who; आभाति – appears; सः – He; अद्वयानन्दलक्षणः – characterised by Bliss, One without a second; अद्वयानन्दरूपः – of the nature of Bliss, One without a second; च – and; प्रत्यग्बोधैकलक्षणः – characterised by the witnessing Consciousness within

39. What appears (ābhāti) as the witness Consciousness within, (the individual Self), is of the nature of Bliss, One without a second; the one that is the Bliss within is none other than the individual Self the witnessing Consciousness within.

The essence behind both jīva (Tvam) and Īśvara (Tat) is 'Bliss without a second' (advayānanda). The expressions of this one Bliss, through the microcosm, avidyā and through the macrocosm, māyā, are the expressions as jīva and Īśvara.

It is very significant and we must note it carefully, how Śaṅkara here, with his precise expressions, specifically hints at the jīva, as the witnessing Consciousness within (pratyag-bodha) and Brahman as the One Bliss without a second (advayānanda). Due to avidyā, the conditioning in the jīva, the individual can experience only the 'awareness' and not the 'Bliss' aspect of Brahman; while, in the supreme Self, 'awareness' cannot be experienced, as there are no objects in it to be illumined, only Bliss and Bliss alone is the nature of Brahman.

In the jīva, the ego, because of its mind-intellect equipment, which is constantly in agitation (vikṣepa), the individual Self can express only its Consciousness (pratyag-bodha), and never the Bliss (advayānanda) nature of the supreme Self. The Brahman is realised when the equipments are all transcended. Therefore it is a state wherein there are no whirls of objects-emotions-thoughts for the Consciousness to illumine. Naturally, the supreme Self is indicated here as Bliss without a second (advayānanda). When these equipments are removed, it is now logically clear that the jīva, in its essential nature, is also pure Bliss, as the Brahman.

What happens when this identity between 'Thou' and 'That' is realised, is explained in the following verse.

इत्थमन्योन्यतादात्म्यप्रतिपत्तिर्यदा भवेत्।
अब्रह्मत्वं त्वमर्थस्य व्यावर्तेत तदैव हि ॥४०॥

itthamanyonyatādātmyapratipattiryadā bhavet,
abrahmatvaṁ tvamarthasya vyāvarteta tadaiva hi. (40)

इत्थम् – in this way; **अन्योन्यतादात्म्यप्रतिपत्तिः** – comprehension of mutual identity; **यदा** – when; **भवेत्** – is; **अब्रह्मत्वम्** – not being Brahman; **त्वम्** – Thou; **अर्थस्य** – of the meaning; **व्यावर्तेत** – shall end; **तदा** – then; **एव हि** – immediately

40. When, as explained above, the mutual identity between the two words 'Thou' and 'That' is comprehended, then the idea 'I am not Brahman' entertained by 'Thou' shall immediately end.

As explained in the above verses so far (ittham), when a seeker first comprehends that the identity of jīva (Thou) and the Self (That) is the depth-meaning of the Mahāvākya, and so when he realises that these two factors are in essence one and the same, then the spiritual ignorance, avidyā, ends. Non-apprehension of the true nature of the supreme Self, and the consequent misapprehension that 'I am the limited ego'- the doer (kartā) and the enjoyer (bhoktā) – should also cease totally. The feeling that 'I am not Brahman' that illumines the very ego, 'Thou' in me, will immediately cease to confuse the seeker in me.

Along with the true apprehension of the real nature of the individual 'Self' jīva, as the very witnessing Consciousness, the misconceived notion that the term 'That' (Tat) in the Mahāvākya is some unseen, unknown, unknowable mighty power, that rules the universe as Jagadīśvara should also cease. The right spiritual realisation immediately will flood the understanding of the seeker: 'That' (Tat) of the Mahāvākya indicates the pure Brahman, ever uncontaminated by the māyā delusions.

The realisation of distinction (bheda jñāna) is the source of all sorrows of saṁsāra of the individual ego. When this sense of distinction between jīva and Īśvara is merged, the bheda jñāna, (which itself is avidyā) the spiritual ignorance, ends in an immediate spiritual revelation of Truth, culminating in a subjective awakening. The ignorance-reared individual ego, in its ignorance can claim, maintain and suffer its own illusory sorrows only as long as it has not awakened to realise its true and real nature as the pure Brahman.

The recognition of a sense of separateness and distinction causes the painful sense of alienation from the world. Then the ego starts its illusory, madly frightening fight with the world of multiplicity, sprung out of its own delusions and finds at every turn its helplessness against the mighty forces of the vast universe spread all around it. At the rediscovery in a personal, intimate experience, 'Thou' and 'That' are both identical, all illusions get at one stroke lifted. Illusions end. The ego sense merges to disappear into the vision of the one blissful Self, eternal, the Brahman.

Then, what?, Śaṅkara explains:

तदर्थस्य च पारोक्ष्यं यद्येवं किं ततः शृणु ।
पूर्णानन्दैकरूपेण प्रत्यग्बोधोऽवतिष्ठते ॥४१ ॥

tadarthasya ca pārokṣyaṁ yadyevaṁ kiṁ tataḥ śṛṇu,
pūṇārnandaikarūpeṇa pratyagbodho'vatiṣṭhate. (41)

तदर्थस्य – of meaning of the term 'That'; पारोक्ष्यम् – hidden (deep); यदि – if; एवम् – as said; किम् – what; ततः – then; शृणु – listen; पूर्णानन्दैकरूपेण – as all-full one mass of Bliss; प्रत्यग्बोधः – witnessing Consciousness; अवतिष्ठते – remains

41. If, as said, the depth-meaning of the term 'That' is 'mass of Bliss without a second' and 'Thou' is the 'witnessing Consciousness' then what? Listen: the inner Self, the Consciousness that illumines all thoughts, remains as the all-full, One mass of Bliss without a second.

The teacher himself raises a doubt for the student and answers it for his edification. In case, as we have been told so far, the jīva and the Īśvara are identical, then what? If this be, at this juncture, your valid doubt, you please listen. I shall explain the witnessing Consciousness (pratyak bodha), which is the depth meaning of jīva (Tvam) will be discovered and realised in an internal experience as ever-full (pūrṇa) and of the nature of one mass of Bliss, One without a second which is the depth-meaning of Īśvara (That).

It was already indicated that the individualised Self, the jīva, can experience only the Consciousness playing within (pratyak bodha) and not the One Bliss mass (advayānanda), which is the nature of Brahman. In Brahman there is no Consciousness as we now know it. We can comprehend only Consciousness of things. In the one infinite Brahman there is nothing for its Consciousness to illuminate. The supreme Self is 'objectless Consciousness' and so not Consciousness as we now comprehend it.

The individual Self, jīva, because of the constant agitations in its mind, can never remain without objects to illumine, and so knows nothing of the peace and bliss of pure Brahman. The supreme Self is the 'one mass of Bliss without a second (pūrṇa-ānanda-eka-rūpa), without Consciousness as we now know it.

When, as explained in the previous verse, the identity between jīva and Īśvara is apprehended in a flash and immediate experience, the student apprehended Brahman, as the 'One bliss without a second' (ānanda-eka-rūpa).

What is the exact contribution of the great statement in bringing the essential identity between 'Thou' and 'That' is being explained in the following verse. The direct meaning of 'Thou' and 'That' are rejected and we accept the indirect meaning of these two suggestive words in the following two verses.

तत्त्वमस्यादिवाक्यं च तादात्म्यप्रतिपादने ।
लक्ष्यौ तत्त्वंपदार्थौं द्वावुपादाय प्रवर्तते ॥४२ ॥

tattvamasyādivākyaṁ ca tādātmyapratipādane,
lakṣyau tattvaṁpadārthau dvāvupādāya pravartate. (42)

तत्त्वमस्यादिवाक्यम् – statements like 'That Thou Art'; च – and; तादात्म्यप्रतिपादने – in the establishment of identity; लक्ष्यौ – indicative; तत्त्वम्पदार्थौं – the meaning of the terms 'That' and 'Thou'; द्वौ – two; उपादाय – bringing forward; प्रवर्तते – engage in

42. The great statements, like 'That Thou Art' established the identity of what is meant by the two terms 'Thou' and 'That' in the deeper indicative meaning.

The indicative meaning (lakṣyārtha) of 'That' was established as the mass of Bliss without a second (advayānanda) and 'Thou' as the witnessing Consciousness within (pratyak bodha). The meanings are accepted on discovering and experiencing the total identity between 'Thou' and 'That'. Naturally, in this process, the direct meanings (vācyārtha) of the terms, 'Thou' as 'jīva' and 'That' as 'Īśvara' were rejected. Then alone the total identity got established.

Vedānta is addressed to the most intelligent students who have cleansed and purified their intellect and so are capable of deep ponderings, subtle visions, and in-depth experiences. To the best among them is given these great declarations (Mahāvākya) for their constant and continuous contemplation. Such sensitive and subtle intellects alone will be able to reject the false and accept the real. An inherent inner strength of vision and meditation is necessary to make these subtle and correct discrimination, reject the grosser and obvious meaning, delve deeper into the greater and ampler suggestiveness in the Mahāvākya.

हित्वा द्वौ शबलौ वाच्यौ वाक्यं वाक्यार्थबोधने ।
यथा प्रवर्ततेऽस्माभिस्तथा व्याख्यातमादरात् ॥४३ ॥

hitvā dvau śabalau vācyau vākyaṁ vākyārthabodhane,
yathā pravartate'smābhistathā vyākhyātamādarāt. (43)

हित्वा – having discarded; द्वौ – two; शबलौ – qualified; वाच्यौ – meanings; वाक्यम् – statement; वाक्यार्थबोधने – in revealing the meaning of the statement; यथा – just as; प्रवर्तते – engage in; अस्माभिः – by us; तथा – so; व्याख्यातम् – commented; आदरात् – carefully

43. How the great statement discards the two qualified meanings and reveals what it really means – this we have carefully commented upon already.

In the Mahāvākya 'That Thou Art' the direct word meanings of the pair – 'That' as Īśvara and 'Thou' as jīva – were qualified meanings (śabalau vācyau). Īśvara was qualified by omniscience,[1] known by indirect Knowledge[2], omnipotence[3] and jīva was

[1] sarvajñatva

[2] parokṣatva

[3] pareśatva

qualified by doership[1], enjoyership[2], joy[3], sorrow[4] and such other dharmas.

We did reject these direct meanings of the words 'Tat' and 'Tvam' and explained the deeper suggestive meanings: the 'Tvam' as the witnessing Consciousness within and the 'Tat' as Consciousness Infinite - the Brahman. Thus is their total and complete identity explained.

The law of commentary prescribes, both by tradition and by natural demand of the intellect that only where direct word meanings are not satisfactory, depth-meanings are to be sought. This is faithfully followed in this simple looking booklet (*Vākya vṛtti*) discussing the silent import of the scriptural statements.

The great statement has three words, 'That Thou Art'; the first two words indicate Īśvara and the jīva, and the last word 'Art' (Asi) clearly roars

---

[1] kartṛtva

[2] bhoktṛtva

[3] sukha

[4] duḥkha

the idea of their total identity with each other. Now, direct word meaning of 'That' (Īśvara) and 'Thou' (jīva), are not adequate meanings to clearly serve and bring out the full significance of them 'Art' (Asi), which suggests the mutual identity between Īśvara and jīva.

The individualised Self (jīva) is Brahman conditioned by the inner equipment – mind and intellect, and it is always riddled with the illusory vanities of 'I am the doer' and 'I am the enjoyer' attitudes. The universal 'Self' (Īśvara) is again Brahman conditioned by māyā and is the Creator of the cosmos, omnipotent and ominscient. Thus, both are equally conditioned by, no doubt, different equipments. They both have different capabilities and capacities. So they both can never be identical.

Thus, direct word meanings of 'That' and 'Thou' will contradict their total identity with each other, so eloquently hinted at by the term 'Art' (Asi) in the Mahāvākya. Therefore, we must consider the depth-meaning of these terms and recognise 'Tvam' as the witnessing Consciousness and 'Tat' as the supreme Brahman. Immediately, then we can recognise their mutual identity.

By accepting the direct word meanings, the statement will palpably contradict the ṛṣi's intimate personal experience in the state of Brahman. Therefore, we are compelled to take the depth-meaning so delicately indicated by the suggestive import of the terms 'That' and 'Thou'.

To establish this contention, Ācārya Śaṅkara briefly explains the direct word meaning of the word 'Thou'.

आलम्बनतयाभाति योऽस्मत्प्रत्ययशब्दयोः ।
अन्तःकरणसंभिन्नबोधः स त्वंपदाभिधः ॥४४ ॥

ālambanatayābhāti yo'smatpratyayaśabdayoḥ,
antaḥkaraṇasambhinnabodhaḥ sa tvampadābhidhaḥ. (44)

आलम्बनतया – as the object; आभाति – shines; यः – which; अस्मत्प्रत्ययशब्दयोः – of the idea and the word 'I'; अन्तःकरणसम्भिन्नबोधः – Consciousness expressing in the inner equipment; सः – that; त्वम्पदाभिधः – known by the term 'Thou'

44. That which shines, as the object of the idea and the word 'I' is Consciousness expressing in the inner equipments. This is the direct word meaning of 'Thou' (Tvam).

Both the ideas behind the first person singular and the meaning of the word 'I' indicate the conscious thought bundle within, the very subject in me, who experiences all my outer environments and also all the inner happenings in me. The thoughts in me, bathed in the light of Consciousness, become the sentient individual entity 'I'. In the absence of either of them, thoughts or Consciousness, the ego 'I' cannot come into the play. The egocentric entity 'I' comes to dance to the prevailing moods of my mind and also to the endless tunes sung by my thoughts.

Since the mind-intellect inner equipment is limited, I feel ever limited, bound, the victim of my own urges, desires, passions and these are often determined by my environment, over which I have no control at all.

This is the direct word meaning (vacyārtha) of the term 'Thou' the jīva.

In the following verse, the direct word meaning of the term 'That' as Īśvara is elaborated.

मायोपाधिर्जगद्योनिः सर्वज्ञत्वादिलक्षणः ।
पारोक्ष्यशबलः सत्याद्यात्मकस्तत्पदाभिधः ॥४५॥

māyopādhirjagadyoniḥ sarvajñatvādilakṣaṇaḥ,
pārokṣyaśabalaḥ satyādyātmakastatpadābhidhaḥ. (45)

मायोपाधिः – which is expressed through māyā; जगद्योनिः – cause of the universe; सर्वज्ञत्वादिलक्षणः – which is described as omniscient and so on; पारोक्ष्यशबलः – which is known indirectly only; सत्याद्यात्मकः – of the nature of Existence and so on; तत्पदाभिधः – known by the term 'That'

45. The Consciousness that is expressed through māyā, which then becomes the 'cause of the universe' which is described as omniscient, and so on; that which is known only indirectly (mediate); which is having the nature of Existence and so on – that Īśvara is the word meaning of the term 'That'.

Īśvara is the Supreme, expressing through the total vāsanās, the māyā. Naturally, He has an equipment to condition Himself[1] and He has microcosmic

[1] māyā

bodies[1] and therefore three types of ego centres.[2] It is Iśvara again who entertained the desire divine; 'I the One, shall become[3] the many.'

Therefore, He with His thoughts (saṅkalpa) created the universe, then desiring to experience, entered the created and became the creature.

All the time as Lord of the universe, Jagadīśvara, He is Master of His māyā, and so He is free, ominipotent and omniscient in His constant awareness of His true nature as Existence-Knowledge. This is the word meaning of the term 'That' in the great statement.

After thus indicating the direct word meaning of these terms in the above two verses, the Ācārya demonstrates how these two meanings cannot prove their mutual identity. He, therefore, justifies the acceptance of the suggestive meanings of the words employed in the Mahāvākya.

---

[1] Virāta, Hiraṇyagarbha, Avyakta are His bodies.

[2] Vaiśvānara; Sūtrātmā; Antaryāmī.

[3] *eko'haṁ bahusyāmiti*

प्रत्यक्परोक्षतैकस्य सद्वितीयत्वपूर्णता ।
विरुध्यते यतस्तस्माल्लक्षणा सम्प्रवर्तते ॥४६ ॥

pratyakparokṣataikasya sadvitīyatvapūrṇatā,
virudhyate yatastasmāllakṣaṇā sampravartate. (46)

प्रत्यक्परोक्षता – quality of being mediately and immediately known; एकस्य – of one (and the same factor); सद्वितीयत्वपूर्णता – the qualities of 'absolute oneness' and 'existence of duality'; विरुध्यते – becomes contrary; यः – since; तस्मात् – hence; लक्षणा – explanation by implication; सम्प्रवर्तते – assume (accept)

46. In case we insist upon the identity of 'That' and 'Thou' based upon the word meaning of these terms, then for one and the same factor we will have to attribute a contrary nature: the quality of being mediately and immediately known and also insist on qualities of existence of duality, and also of 'absolute oneness' for one and the same factor. Identity between such contrariness is impossible; hence the suggestive meaning, 'the explanation by implication' has to be accepted.

Identity can only be between two things of similar qualities and if we accept the word meaning (vacyārtha) of the terms employed in the Mahāvākya, then we will never be able to arrive at any logical possibility of their identity.

Jīva is experienced by itself in everyone; Īśvara is beyond our direct experience. How can there be identity between them?

Maybe the Mahāvākya is not indicating any identity between them. This cannot be true, because of what has been said in the Upaniṣad leading up to the declaration, 'That Thou Art.' The father was anxiously teaching his son-disciple the oneness and absolute identity between the supreme Self and the essence in the individual Self.

Thus, by the word meaning of 'Thou' (jīva) and 'That' (Īśvara) the identity between them cannot be discovered. Therefore, we are compelled to delve into the suggestive meaning of these two terms and recognise them as 'Thou' meaning the witness Consciousness in the individual bosom and 'That' meaning the one mass of Bliss without a second

– the Brahman. This process of understanding the depth-meaning and arriving at the indicative suggestiveness in the words of a statement is known as 'lakṣaṇa'.

What then is the suggestive meaning of a word or a statement? How do we arrive at it? Śaṅkara defines the lakṣaṇa methods (indirect meaning) in the following verse:

मानान्तरविरोधे तु मुख्यार्थस्य परिग्रहे।
मुख्यार्थेनाविनाभूते प्रतीतिर्लक्षणोच्यते ॥४७॥

mānāntaravirodhe tu mukhyārthasya parigrahe,
mukhyārthenāvinābhūte pratītirlakṣaṇocyate. (47)

मानान्तरविरोधे – on being inconsistent with what is pointed out by other proofs and evidences; तु – however (if); मुख्यार्थस्य – of the direct word meaning; परिग्रहे – on accepting; मुख्यार्थेन – with the direct word meaning; अविनाभूते – with the sense (meaning) which is consistent; प्रतीतिः – intelligently suggested by itself (the terms); लक्षणा – suggestive meaning; उच्यते – said

47. If the direct word meaning throws up an inconsistency with what is pointed out by other proofs and evidences, the sense consistent with its word meaning that is intelligently suggested by the terms is to be accepted, this is its suggestive meaning (lakṣaṇā).

When the direct word meaning (vācyārtha) can say only something brutally self-contradictory (like ice is hot) to our personal experience and / or other established sources of knowledge (māna-antara-virodha), then the sense that intelligently suggests itself by the words in a statement, becomes acceptable and this is its suggestive meaning (lakṣyārtha). Very often thus, the direct dictionary meaning will have to be dropped ('He consumed a mountain of oranges') and its subtle import is to be taken (large, unimaginably large, quantity of oranges was consumed). This process is called (lakṣaṇā-vṛtti). This lakṣaṇā is of three kinds: 'reject method' (jaha-lakṣaṇā), 'accept method' (ajaha- lakṣaṇā), and 'reject-accept method' (jahājaha-lakṣaṇā).

The 'reject method' is employed in correctly understanding a statement as 'my house is right on the sea.' Here the direct word meaning would be a palpable foolishness, as a house cannot float on the oceanic waters. Therefore, we reject the direct meaning of the heaving ocean and understand the statement as 'the house is nearest to the sea.' This is jaha-lakṣaṇā. This cannot be used in arriving at the significance of the Mahāvākya.

The 'accept method' is made use of in arriving at the meaning of a statement like 'the red ran' or 'the guns marched.' Here the direct meaning will point to something impossible and therefore, while retaining the direct meaning, we accept a new factor suggested by the statement and understand it as 'the red horse ran' or 'the gunmen marched.' This is ajaha-lakṣaṇā; this also cannot be employed in arriving at the true meaning of the Mahāvākya.

The 'reject-accept method' is commissioned to explore the meaning of a statement as 'this is that child of mine.' The term 'this' is used for something standing near at hand, right now, and 'that' is used for something far off, in the past, away from the speaker and the listener. 'This young man with me now, so well grown-up and hefty in body, is that baby whom you used to handle, then, in the past, when the child was so tiny and slender in body.' Here the time, size and nature of the body are all rejected, and the baby that was then, is recognised as this grown-up young man. The individual's identity is accepted; but one part is rejected and another part is accepted. This is jahājaha-lakṣaṇā. This method is made use of in arriving at the secret import of the great statement, 'That Thou Art.'

Of these three methods which is to be accepted for comprehending the meaning of the great statement 'That Thou Art' is being explained now in the following verse.

तत्त्वमस्यादिवाक्येषु लक्षणा भागलक्षणा ।
सोऽयमित्यादिवाक्यस्थपदयोरिव नापरा ॥४८ ॥

tattvamasyādivākyeṣu lakṣaṇā bhāgalakṣaṇā,
so'yamityādivākyasthapadayoriva nāparā. (48)

तत्त्वमस्यादिवाक्येषु – in the statements like 'That Thou Art'; लक्षणा – method; भागलक्षणा – the reject-accept method; सः अयम् इत्यादिवाक्यस्थपदयोः – in the terms present in the sentences like 'He is this man' and so on; इव – as; न – no; अपरा – another (other)

48. In the statement like 'That Thou Art' the reject-accept method is to be employed as in the sentence 'He is this man.' No other method can be applied.

The 'accept-reject method' is also called in Vedānta as bhāga-tyāga-lakṣaṇā. Here we give up in part the direct word meaning (both the child that was and the young man that is) and we arrive at the exact import of the statement. In both 'Thou' and 'That' the principle of Consciousness is the same, only the conditionings are different in each of them.

By rejecting the microcosmic and macrocosmic equipments of jīva and Īśvara, what is left over is the one essential Self which sports as both the witnessing Consciousness within, and the Brahman, the sole substratum for the entire universe of names and forms.

This reject-accept method (bhaga-tyāga lakṣaṇā) alone can be profitably used in understanding the true significance of the statements of Vedas, 'That Thou Art!'[1] 'I am Brahman!'[2] and so on. When the conditionings are removed from jīva and Īśvara, the pure Consciousness, sporting as ego in the individual and as Lord of the universe, is recognised as the one supreme Brahman, the one mass of Bliss without a second.

Even after gaining this exact understanding of the depth-meaning of the great statement, the identity between the individual Self and the supreme Self will not easily get effectively firm in our apprehension. What should we then do? 'student of Vedānta need not despair' – says Ācārya Śaṅkara.

1 tattvamasi

2 *ahaṁ brahmāsmi*

अहं ब्रह्मेतिवाक्यार्थबोधो यावद्दृढीभवेत्।
शमादिसहितस्तावदभ्यसेच्छ्रवणादिकम्॥४९॥

ahaṁ brahmetivākyārthabodho yāvaddṛḍhībhavet,
śamādisahitastāvadabhyasecchravaṇādikam. (49)

अहं ब्रह्म इति वाक्यार्थबोधः – the personal experience of the meaning of the sentence 'I am Brahman'; यावत् – until; दृढीभवेत् – gained (becomes firm); शमादिसहितः – along with self-control and so on; तावद् – so long; अभ्यसेत् – practise; श्रवणादिकम् – listening and so on

49. Until the direct personal experience of 'I am Brahman' is gained, we must live values of self-control, practise listening to teachers, reading scriptures and doing daily reflection and meditation upon those ideas.

The book knowledge is the final goal, the be-all and the end-all of study, is true only in the objective sciences. In the subjective science of spiritual unfoldment, the knowledge of the text is but a beginning; the final fulfilment is in the seeker's own direct, personal experience, 'Brahman am I.'

Often, it can so happen to the seekers that they have intellectually understood the import of the spiritual experience of the spiritual factor, the one Essence. To them Ācārya Śaṅkara prescribes the only logical way of life – the sādhanā programme.

Those who have not cultivated in themselves the necessary preconditions can never soar high into the subtler realms of their own inner personality. The values in the life to be lived are explained elaborately by Śaṅkara in his *Vivekacūḍamaṇi*.[1]

There are many direct psychological obstacles that come to block our final spiritual experience. When we try to sincerely and intelligently study the various statements of different scriptures, intellectually, we may come to the conclusion that they make but a confusing array of self-contradictory declarations. From these, many intellectual doubts (saṁśaya) can arise.

Again, subjectively, our mind's lust for sense objects is so natural with us now, that the hungry inner personality may try and even convince us that

[1] *Vivekacūḍamaṇi*-17-27

the theme of the scriptures is unnatural and contrary to life's true impulses (viparīta bhāvanā). Again and again we must read, study, listen, reflect and try to digest the scriptural thoughts and ideas. When by this process of study, reflecting and mutual discussions among students, our recognition of the one Self becomes clearer, then the sense of contrariness and the consequent perplexities (viparīta bhāvanā) will end.

Cultivate devotion for the Lord; worship the Lord of your heart; spend time and energy in the selfless service of mankind and the world around, this is to be undertaken as a worship of the Lord. These can help the inner equipment to unfold and glow with brightness, peace and cheer. The steadiness in meditation will thus increase.

The various personality adjustments recommended by Śaṅkara in the *Vivekacūḍamaṇi* are all, in fact, of the best psychological adjustments in effectively facing our personal inner problems and outer challenges. Without these intelligent adjustments in our value system, mental dissipations cannot, in fact, be reduced. A dissipated mind will never have the power of penetration and the alertness necessary for fruitful study and effective contemplation.

A student who has thus carefully cultivated his inner equipment can consistently pursue the study of the scriptures and go deeper and deeper into their significance with his own sincere reflections. This prepares the seeker for a more and more rewarding meditation. Finally, he shall explode his ego-sense, gain a breakthrough and re-enter into the infinite state of pure Brahman. Until this personally intimate, totally subjective experience of the supreme Self is gained, Vedānta study is not to be considered as fulfilled.

When once the direct experience of Brahman is gained through the grace of the teacher and the blessing of the scriptures, what exactly happens to the seeker? Ādi Śaṅkara declares:

श्रुत्याचार्यप्रसादेन दृढो बोधो यदा भवेत्।
निरस्ताशेषसंसारनिदानः पुरुषस्तदा ॥५०॥

śrutyācāryaprasādena dṛḍho bodho yadā bhavet,
nirastāśeṣasaṁsāranidānaḥ puruṣastadā. (50)

श्रुत्याचार्यप्रसादेन – through the grace of a teacher and the scriptures; दृढः – clear (firm); बोधः – experience; यथा – as soon as; भवेत् – becomes; निरस्ताशेषसंसारनिदानः – free from all ignorance which is the cause for the world of plurality or transmigration; पुरुषः – person; तदा – then

50. Through the grace of a spiritual teacher, when a seeker gains a clear and direct experience of the supreme Self as expounded in the scriptures, he, the Realised, becomes free from all ignorance, which is the foundation for the entire experience of this world of plurality.

By the grace of a spiritual teacher (Guru), when a seeker studies in depth the Upaniṣads, his spiritual ignorance (avidyā) ends. This ignorance expresses as the non-apprehension of Reality, and provides misapprehensions of the Truth behind the universe. When he gains a direct, personal experience of this supreme state of pure Consciousness his non-apprehension ends in his apprehension of the Truth. When non-apprehension ends all misapprehensions created by it must also cease to exist.

It was the misapprehensions of the body, mind and intellect (BMI) and their objects, emotions and thoughts (OET), that provided existence and power to the imaginary phantom in us, the sense of individuality, the jīva. It is the jīva that went through its illusory sufferings of limitations, helpless sorrows, endless privations, and maintained a tragic sense of alienation in his vast, wide world, recognised by it, in its own fabulous delusions. Where the ego disappears into the vision of the supreme Brahman in an intimate, direct experience, the illusory world of finitude ends with all its imperfections, death, decay, change and endless passions.

The life of shocks and pains, of births and deaths, of fears and anxieties is called saṁsāra.[1]

[1] saṁsarati iti saṁsāraḥ – The plane of existence where everything comes and goes, everything appears and disappears is called saṁsāra.

The accessories of the jīva's sorrows of saṁsāra are but its own subjective desires, passions, lust, pride, prejudices and so on. All these will cease to torture the individual when the sense of individuality ends in the unique experience of the supreme Brahman.

Then what happens to the seeker? Śaṅkara continues with a rare poetic vigour.

विशीर्णकार्यकरणो भूतसूक्ष्मैरनावृतः ।
विमुक्तकर्मनिगडः सद्य एव विमुच्यते ॥५१॥

viśīrṇakāryakaraṇo bhūtasūkṣmairanāvṛtaḥ,
vimuktakarmanigaḍaḥ sadya eva vimucyate. (51)

विशीर्णकार्यकरणः – gross and subtle bodies; भूतसूक्ष्मैः – by the subtle and gross; अनावृतः – unconditioned; विमुक्तकर्मनिगडः – released from the shackle (fetter) of actions; सद्य एव – immediately; विमुच्यते – liberated

51. No more conditioned by his gross and subtle bodies, free from the embrace of the gross and subtle elements, released from the charm of actions, such a man gets immediately Liberated.

The five gross elements in their combinations constitute the gross outer world of names and forms, including our gross bodies. The subtle elements go into the make-up of the mind and thoughts, including the sense stimuli provided by the outer objects[1] The outer gross body and its objects form the 'effects' (kārya) of the vāsanās in the individual and the inner subtle body, consisting of our mind and intellect, becomes the entire equipment (karaṇa)[2] of experience. They together, form the 'tool kit' with us for contacting the world of plurality and for accomplishing our experience.

To identify with them is to live and express as mere physical, mental and intellectual personalities. These triple aspects, together, constitute the individual ego in us. This ego in its unique Experience Divine merges itself in the Brahman. All its identifications cease and the sense of individuality disappears.

This ego alone, had the arrogant vanity of 'doership' (kartṛtva bhāva) and the 'enjoyership' (bhoktṛtva bhāva). It is the ego who did all actions in the past, collected all vāsanās and is now experiencer of the fruits of those actions. When the ego ends, all

[1] The form, colour, smell, taste, touch, sound, and so on are the stimuli that reach our mind from the world of objects, perceived through our sense organs. These stimuli are made up of the subtle elements: the tanmātras.

[2] Tool-kit in us for gathering our experiences in life.

actions must cease; as an absconding criminal, when dead, the warrant of arrest issued against him must, out of necessity become both null and void.

The doer of an action, alone, can be the experiencer of its fruits. The doer-experiencer entity, the ego, the jīva, has now awakened fully from its illusory dream of saṁsāra into the state of Brahman. He would then be unavoidably freed from the chain of action (karma).

To leave the dream is to wake up; to end the ego is to rise above the perceptions and sorrows of the world of multiplicity. There is no interval of time between the birth of knowledge of the supreme Self and the Liberation from the thraldom of the equipment. Such a realised sage, even in the midst of sense objects, cannot be affected as he is fully and entirely released from the realm of subject-object world of finite joys and sorrow.

प्रारब्धकर्मवेगेन जीवन्मुक्तो यदा भवेत्।
किञ्चित्कालमनारब्धकर्मबन्धस्य संक्षये ॥५२॥

prārabdhakarmavegena jīvanmukto yadā bhavet,
kiñcitkālamanārabdhakarmabandhasya saṅkṣaye. (52)

प्रारब्धकर्मवेगेन – due to the force of those actions which have begun to produce their results; **जीवन्मुक्तः** – Liberated while living; **यदा** – when; **भवेत्** – becomes; **किञ्चित्कालम्** – for some time; **अनारब्धकर्मबन्धस्य** – of the bondage of actions that have not begun to produce their results; **संक्षये** – to exhaust

52. The Liberated in life, due to the compelling force of those actions that have to produce their results (prārabdha), remains for some time in order to exhaust them.

Why do we find the Liberated in life (Jīvanmukta) still continuing as a member of the community, often working hard for the spiritual redemption of man? He has transcended his mind and intellect as he has exhausted his vāsanās. The previous verse did assert that such a seeker 'freed from the chain of actions is immediately Liberated.' The answer according to the śāstras is that, with the realisation of 'I am Brahman' all the accumulated karma (sañcita) of the past and the future karmas (āgāmī) to be experienced in the future, are both totally annihilated and erased. But the actions that have begun to yield fruits will have to continue. They have to find their exhaustion in vivid experiences; they are like bullets that have left the gun. It is now too late to regret, no one can catch the hissing bullets in flight and change their course; they have to exhaust themselves.

To live those experiences ordered by prārabdha, the Liberated one continues in his physical form is the explanation that we find in the scriptures.

Śaṅkara himself in his *Vivekacūdamaṇi* had taken up this idea and had exhaustively dealt with it. However, he concludes that it is an explanation given to the dull-witted, who asks the question why a Realised man has a body and all the natural bodily activities.

On the exhaustion of world's prārabdha to be served by such a fully Realised prophetic Master, his body falls off. His experience of Brahman is never broken off at any time. It is the prārabdha of others that drive the Jīvanmukta's form to continue to function for the spiritual edification of the world, for the welfare of man's inner spiritual life.

निरस्तातिशयानन्दं वैष्णवं परमं पदम् ।
पुनरावृत्तिरहितं कैवल्यं प्रतिपद्यते ॥५३ ॥

nirastātiśayānandaṁ vaiṣṇavaṁ paramaṁ padam,
punarāvṛttirahitaṁ kaivalyaṁ pratipadyate. (53)

निरस्तातिशयानन्दम् – never ending immeasurable Bliss; **वैष्णवम्** – of Viṣṇu; **परमम्** – Supreme; **पदम्** – abode; **पुनरावृत्तिरहितम्** – wherein there is no return; **कैवल्यम्** – state of absolute Oneness; **प्रतिपद्यते** – gains/reaches

53. The Liberated in life comes to gain the state of absolute Oneness, the never ending immeasurable Bliss, called the supreme abode of Viṣṇu, wherein there is no return.

That which never ends or sets (nirasta) is called eternal Infinite. The liberated in life has finally arrived at this never ending immeasurable Bliss called 'the supreme abode of Viṣṇu.' Here, it is not to be understood as Lord Viṣṇu's residence in heaven, the realm called Vaikuṇṭha, but is the supreme state which is Viṣṇu, the all-pervading.

On awakening to this state of Godhood – the Brahman, there is no return to the old misconceptions arising out of the body, mind and intellect identifications and the consequent limited life of sufferings and tensions lived by the delusory ego (jīva).

This final destination of evolution, the state of no-return, is called kaivalya in Vedānta. That which has no distinction in itself, or with others, is called kevala; that state of homogenous Brahman, the One without a second, is called the state of kaivalya. The limited in life attains to this state of Bliss and becomes one with Brahman. This, indeed, is the depth-meaning of the great statement, 'That Thou Art.'

Om Tat Sat

Alphabetical Index to ślokas